Foot in the Door

A Lindell Prequel

Marie James

Copyright

Synopsis

Flirting isn't hard.

And before that stupid parent/teacher conference, I would've called myself an expert.

A smirk, a wink, a little inviting body language, and I was in.

McKenna Kaiser, my nephew's new kindergarten teacher, seems to be immune to all three.

There are a million words I would use to describe her: perfect, gorgeous, kind, to name a few.

But after leaving the meeting, only one word came to mind: unimpressed.

Sticking a foot in my mouth isn't physically possible, yet here I am chewing on a size twelve wingtip.

After a crash and burn of epic proportions, I would usually walk away and count my losses.

But I can't stop thinking about her.

I know I can change her mind about me.

I just need to get my foot in the door.

Chapter 1

McKenna

"Stop that!" I hiss.

"What?" My best friend, Courtney chuckles. "It's hilarious. So funny, that I'm pretty sure you're lying."

"Not you. Garrett is being a pest." I swat at the ferret again as he tries to dip his paw into the bowl of cereal on my lap. "And you'll see when you get here. The entire town is nuts."

"I don't see living in an eclectic town as a problem."

"It's not a problem."

"But you just said that you avoid the hippie store because he makes you uncomfortable."

"Stop it, you heathen. Go eat your own food." Garrett backs away but keeps his eyes on my food. "Hippie Jones owns The Devil's Lettuce. It's a gift shop and herbal remedy store, not a hippie store."

"Now you're just splitting hairs."

"I'm not used to it is all. The town is so small. Everyone knows everyone else, and I stick out like a sore thumb."

"It can't be that bad."

"One of my students came to class the other day and told me that I didn't plant my daffodil bulbs deep enough. Who is paying so close attention that they know how deep the dang holes were?"

"Nosy neighbors?"

"Nosy town."

"Any hot guys?"

At this I have to scoff. I've been in town for two weeks. I replaced a kindergarten teacher that had to go out of state to take care of an ill relative.

"None."

Silence fills the line before Courtney speaks again, and I already know she's going to say something off the wall. "It's a college town, right?"

"I'm not dating a college student."

She's right, though. There are tons of young adults roaming around the town, many of them having grown up right here in Lindell, Texas. Austin is about an hour's drive, so I don't know why they chose to stay in this sleepy town instead of sowing their wild oats in the city. If I weren't desperate for a job, I never would've landed here either.

"They're of legal age," she argues.

"I deal with children all day at school. I don't need a barely adult male in my bed, too."

"So, you're just looking for a bed warmer? That's actually perfect. College guys aren't known to stick around the morning after."

I laugh. "You need to stop."

"Are you only avoiding the gift shop?"

She laughed for a solid five minutes when I told her the name of the store, and I know she's avoiding calling it by name again to keep from chuckling, but I can hear the laughter in her voice.

"I'm not really avoiding any place, but I don't think I'll be going to the Brew and Chew any time soon. I wish they—"

"The what?"

"The Brew and Chew. It's a diner and the only place to get decent coffee."

She snorts. "What's your definition of decent?"

"Well, I mean, it's better than the complimentary cups offered at The Fresh Quest Grocer."

"Free coffee? That doesn't happen in the city."

"The people are different down here, but they're nice."

"But you won't go to the Brew and Chew?"

"There's no privacy. The other day I was sitting there enjoying a cup of coffee and an omelet and these two guys approach."

"Hot guys?"

"No, I told you there aren't any hot guys in town. Just listen."

She stays quiet while I relay the story.

For a small town, the food is better than I ever expected. I don't know what kind of seasoning the cook uses, but my omelet is spectacular.

The bell above the door dings, but after a quick glance up, I refocus on my food, considering placing an order for another one to take home and have for dinner later.

"Hey there, gorgeous."

I don't bother looking up. I wouldn't if I were sitting at a café in Dallas where I'm from and some guy approached and thought he could walk in and greet me like this. The guys up there would normally go away, but the presence gets bigger, nearly blocking out all of the natural light coming in from the huge pane-glass windows at the front of the diner.

It forces my hand. Only when I lift my eyes, I'm not looking at one guy pressing his luck, but two.

My gaze darts between the two of them. It's clear they're twins, but the burly guys move as one. They wink as if the act is practiced for a movie, and if it weren't for their thick beards, I imagine a glint of sparkle would reflect off each one's front tooth with how much charm they're attempting to throw my way.

"Can I help you?" I ask.

I wouldn't call them classically handsome because they're like mountain men, but I can see the appeal. This act probably works often for them, but they're just not the type of guy I would ever be interested in.

"Us?" the one on the right asks, his hand sweeping down his unruly beard. "It's always us."

"We're the Tate brothers." The other one winks again, and my eyebrow goes up.

"Okay." I lower my fork to my plate. I'll play along if it means I can get them out of my hair before my food goes cold.

"I'm Ronnie," the guy on the right says before jabbing a meaty finger toward his brother. "He's Donnie."

How original.

"What time do you want us to pick you up?" Donnie asks.

I tilt my head, very sure I missed part of the conversation, but their bright blue eyes just gleam down at me, waiting for an answer.

"I'm not—no, thank you." *Concise and straight to the point, that should work.*

Ronnie looks at Donnie, and Donnie looks back at him. If confusion were pictured in the dictionary, this scene would be perfect.

"We're the Tate brothers," *Ronnie says when he turns his attention back to me.*

"We do everything together." *Donnie's eyebrows waggle, something I thought only possible with cartoon animation, but this guy seems to have mastered it.*

If you're wondering, it looks just as ridiculous now as it does on television.

"Stop!" Courtney roars with laughter.

I give up on my bowl of cereal, placing it on the coffee table and giving Garrett free use of it. He stuck his paw in more than once while I was relaying my last visit to the Brew and Chew to my friend.

I wait for her to calm down and it takes a while after the snorting begins. A smile spreads across my face. My friend is planning to visit soon, and I know she thinks I'm joking, but I couldn't make this stuff up even if I hadn't taken a creative writing class in college.

"Just like that? You were invited into a three-way by two mountain men in the middle of a small-town diner?"

"Just like that, and the entire town is like that."

"How many sexual offers have you gotten?"

"Not in that way," I clarify. "The people just approach and start talking like I've known them their entire lives. It's strange. They have no boundaries."

"They're helpful."

"The Tate brothers were not helpful."

"I don't know, being tag teamed by hunky twins could be fun."

"I never said they were hunky."

"They aren't?"

"I mean, you'd probably find them attractive, but they don't fit the bill for me."

"I can't wait to visit. I have my flight planned."

"Maybe I should come there."

"Nope. Not a chance. I want to see your place, and after these ridiculous stories, I have to see the town. I'm sorry you hate it."

"I don't *hate* it," I rush out, because I don't.

The people are quirky and odd, but they're not only involved in the town's business but also the kids' education. I discovered quickly during school while doing my observation hours at a school in Dallas that many parents aren't involved in their kids' educations. Either they were too busy working to provide for their families, or they saw the school as a childcare facility and didn't want to be bothered with any issue there. If problems arose, it was the teachers' and staff's responsibility to correct the issue rather than a parent getting involved.

That is definitely not the case here in Lindell. More often than not, it's more a matter of making sure to not let people get involved in other parents' kids' education that they don't belong to. More than once I've had to get my principal involved when a parent wants to *help* with more than just their own kids.

"It's growing on me."

"So, no major problems then?"

"Not really." I shrug even though she can't see me. "I'm certain the woman in the front office hates me, but the second grade teacher assures me that Marcy hates everyone."

"I can kick her ass when I come to town, if you need me to."

A grin tugs up the corners of my mouth. I know she would. My best friend is scrappy on a good day and has the ability to go all MMA on a bad one.

"I'll pick you up at the airport."

"I've already rented a car."

"You don't want to be stuck here," I argue.

"You know how work is. I could get a call and have to leave in the middle of the night."

"True," I agree. "So, I'll see you soon?"

"Not even Hippie Jones can keep me away."

We hang up, and I'm left with a grin. Just like I told her, the town isn't bad, it's just different—a complete culture shock going from the bustle of the city to a town that seems to have a hatred for any form of convenience. There isn't a single drive-thru restaurant, and you won't find a chain store within the city limits. Even the gas station has an attendant there to pump your gas and wash your windshield.

It's like I've fallen back into the nineteen fifties, only back then, they had hunks like Robert Redford and Cary Grant. Today, Lindell, Texas is stuck in time with the Tate brothers.

Chapter 2
Kalen

"You come here often?"

Yes, the pickup line is cheesy, but for some reason it makes women laugh. They readily strike up a conversation.

At least they usually do.

But clearly the gorgeous woman standing just inside the front entrance of Lindell Elementary isn't like most women.

She isn't grinning or twirling her hair around her finger as she lets her eyes roam up and down my body.

The frown is unexpected, but since she doesn't slap me in the face, it's something I can work with.

You may think hitting on women at my nephew's school is a little weird, and most of the time that might be the case, but Lindell is a small town, meaning the pickings are slim, as in so slim they're nonexistent.

Letting a gorgeous woman walk by without attempting to get her number would be sheer stupidity on my part, and I'm not stupid very often.

"May I help you?" She plasters a fake-as-hell smile on her pretty lips, and there's no joy in her eyes.

It's like a slap to the face and makes me wonder how many other men in the community have hit on her already.

Anyone who crossed her path would be my guess, including Old Man Hinkle, if she has had any reason to step foot near the post office.

"You like to eat, right?"

Her eyes dart down the front of her shirt before snapping back up to me.

"Excuse me?"

Even the fake smile is no competition for the irritation now showing on her pretty face. Her bright green eyes narrow as she glares at me.

"Not that you're that fat." *What the hell is wrong with me? She isn't fat at all.*

I'm a pro at this. Flirting is second nature to me. I could do it all day, every day. Well, when I get a chance.

I lay it on thick when I need a little extra caffeine at Brew and Chew, the local café.

I'm not opposed to batting my eyelashes at Marlene down at the corner store when I know she's hiding the good snacks in the back.

I've even winked at Peter Stanton when I thought he was going to take the last pecan pie the day before Thanksgiving.

My flirting works. My coffee always has an extra shot of espresso. Marlene grins and waves me toward the back room when she sees me walk in. Hell, Peter sent me a Christmas card last year.

"Excuse me?" she hisses, her cheeks turning a vibrant pink.

"I was asking if—" Her hands go to her hips, one foot turned out in agitation, and I realize this was over before it really began. "Do you know where the front office is?"

She points to a door. The words FRONT OFFICE are across the front, and it's clear she thinks I'm an idiot.

"If you even hint to Marcy that you think she's fat, she'll tear your head off."

She spins around, long blonde hair like a whip behind her, disappearing around the corner, leaving me with my mouth hanging open and a million excuses on the tip of my tongue.

The day just gets worse from here.

Marcy is in a mood of epic proportions, mostly stemming from the time we dated briefly in high school. She had four cats. I'm extremely allergic. She thought it was love. I knew it was borderline anaphylaxis.

She's hated me ever since.

"Well, if it isn't Kalen Alexander," Marcy snarls when I pull open the heavy door leading into the front office. "Are you here to make more little kids cry?"

It was one time, and that kid was already crying before I approached.

I grind my back teeth, something our local dentist wouldn't be happy with, but after catching his wife in bed with the mayor, he doesn't have much free time on his hands these days. Afterall, he has been spending a lot of time replacing the teeth he knocked out.

"Marcy," I say, aiming for casual and light and ending up staying close to the door. Just stepping into the room makes my nose itch. I fight back the urge to sneeze. "Always lovely to see you."

"I'm a busy woman, Kalen. What do you need?"

"Kristina couldn't make the parent/teacher conference, so I'm here."

"Poor kid," Marcy mutters.

"So, if you give me the room number—"

"I need you to complete this form."

She slaps a clipboard on the counter in front of me, making the pen fly halfway across the room.

I want to tell her it was nearly fourteen years ago and that she should let go of the past, but after what happened in the hall moments ago, I know it's best to just keep my mouth shut as I grab the pen from the floor.

When I turn back, she's holding out her hand. "Your driver's license?"

"My—" I roll my lips between my teeth and reach for my wallet. "Is this really necessary? You know who I am."

The town is so small, everyone knows everyone else. The beauty in the hall earlier is the only stranger I've seen outside of work in months, but we get new faces all the time at the college.

"ID is required each time a visitor comes on campus. I don't make the rules, Kalen, but I will follow them."

"And," I look down at the form on the clipboard, "you need my phone number, home and mailing address?"

"The form is required."

I work on completing the form, including my email address as well as two personal references. I've rented a car without giving this much information before. As I hand over the form, I almost open my mouth to remind her that it's for school use only, so she doesn't get any ideas about using it to contact me or sign me up for some weird porn site, but she snaps the thing away from me so hard it makes the tips of my fingers burn.

Marcy is a fight for another day because if she doesn't hurry, I'm going to be late.

"Justin's teacher is in room 114. When was your appointment?"

"Twelve fifteen."

"And you're already late."

"Thank you," I say instead of reminding her that jumping through hoops in a school that has an average of twelve students in each grade is ridiculous.

The familiar yet spicy scent of the hallway as I leave the office is as good as fresh air compared to the tainted, allergy-infested air of the front office.

Traveling familiar halls doesn't bring a sense of nostalgia because I'm late. I hate being late more than anything.

I breathe in with a sense of relief as I put the weird day behind me.

That is until I find room 114 and discover the girl who broke my ability to flirt sitting behind the desk.

When I open the door and her eyes meet mine, I try again.

She slowly blinks at my teasing smile, and it immediately puts me off-kilter.

Yep, still broken.

"You're not Mrs. Eaton."

She frowns further. "Is that another weight joke?"

I want to reach for my phone and swipe through the emails to find the right teacher's name. I pick my nephew up from school most days because my sister works a later shift and can't take off. As a professor at Lindell University, I don't have an afternoon class. Justin started the year with a Mrs. Eaton. I know this for a fact because I attended meet the teacher, and that woman loved me.

"His…" I point to my phone as if she can read my mind. "Justin's teacher's name is Mrs. Easton."

"Was."

"Huh?"

"*Was*. Mrs. Easton took a leave of absence to tend to a sick family member. I'm McKenna Kaiser, her replacement for the remainder of the year. You're here for Justin Alexander?"

I nod, trying to refocus my attention on her words rather than the shiny lips producing them.

"Kalen Alexander," I tell her, approaching and holding my hand out.

She looks down at my proffered hand but doesn't reach for it.

"With the display in the hallway and your lack of listening skills, I can see where Justin gets it from. Please have a seat, Mr. Alexander. We have a lot to discuss, and you're already ten minutes late."

I obey the best I can, but folding myself into the tiny, blue chair is nearly impossible.

"Let's talk about Justin catcalling the little girls on the playground, shall we?"

Chapter 3

McKenna

"I don't think it should be a problem. The last teacher didn't have an issue with it."

I look at the parent sitting across from me, and I just can't focus.

I've been doing parent/teacher conferences nearly all week, squeezing them into my conference period.

They've all gone well, except the one before this one.

Kalen Alexander, father of Justin Alexander.

The same fool who not only insulted me right before the meeting but also the very same man who has the audacity to be the best-looking guy I've ever seen.

As in... ever.

Not just in Lindell, but like every place I've ever been.

Hot. Smoking. Fine as hell.

And of course he has to be a jerk with his luscious dark hair, bright blue eyes, and pillowy perfect lips.

And married, I remind myself.

Yeah, that's a huge issue.

"Well?" the parent in front of me prods.

"I'm sorry. What were you saying?"

And this is another reason I dislike the man. I can't focus.

"The hat," Mrs. Hinkle reminds me.

"The hat needs to stay at home." I'm sure I've already said this.

"It's his thinking cap," she argues.

"It stinks—there's an odor coming from it. It's distracting the kids."

The truth is the hat reeks, and Sammy is getting picked on daily for it.

"It's his thinking cap."

"I don't mind him wearing a hat, but maybe something a little less animal-like."

Her eyes narrow, her weight shifting in the chair, and I can tell she's about to get her hackles up. Most people in town are sugary sweet, but mess with one of their little cubs and momma bear will turn ferocious in a heartbeat.

"Are you one of those PETA people?"

"No, ma'am," I assure her. I may not be from a small town, but I am from the south, and no stranger to the idea of hunting. "I don't have an issue with the hat formerly being a raccoon. The issue is the stench coming off it. It's distracting everyone in class."

"He skinned it himself."

At five? Lord, what hole have I fallen into?

"He's very proud of it," I agree.

She beams as if I've agreed to let it go.

I lean in, looking around the room even though we're alone in here, but it serves me well as the universal sign that I'm fixing to share something with her I don't want anyone else to know. Just as I suspected she would, Mrs. Hinkle leans in closer as well, a wide smile on her face. Gossip, I've learned, is like currency in this small town.

"I shouldn't be saying this." I pause, looking over her shoulder for dramatic affect. "But, since Sammy is one of my favorite students…"

Honestly, I really like all of my students. Even Justin Alexander, who's dad is a sexy idiot. Actually, that kid may be my favorite if I had to choose. He's ridiculously funny, and I can count on him for a good laugh since the craziest things come out of his little mouth.

"I'm not going to say who, so please don't ask, but one of the kids came down with lice."

Mrs. Hinkle hisses, her hand automatically going to her throat, and I bet she's missing her Sunday pearls right now because she has nothing to clutch. It's as if I've confessed to a mortal sin.

"I know that Sammy is very proud of his hat because he likes to pass it around and let his peers try it on. Now, I've kept it from the kid in question, but if he keeps sharing, it's only a matter of time."

She nods as if I've disclosed top secret information that's going to save her family from a major issue, one that would take more than a visit to the pharmacy and a night with a nit comb.

"So, I just want him to be safe."

She nods, her head bobbing aggressively. "I bet it's that Nichols kid."

"It's not."

"Then it's the Graves boy. His momma had lice when we were in school."

"It's not," I repeat. "And I said I wouldn't tell you."

She looks at me expectantly, as if staring me down will make my lips loosen, but other than Kalen Alexander, the only thing I can concentrate on right now is not lifting my hand to scratch behind my ear. What is it about talking about lice that always makes my head itch?

I give Mrs. Hinkle a small smile.

"Will you ask him to keep the hat at home?"

"Of course," she readily agrees. "I don't want an infested house. Do you know how hard it is to get rid of lice?"

"Very difficult," I agree. "Thank you so much. It helps me immensely and keeps the other kids safe."

I feel like a jerk using something as common as lice and treating it like the bubonic plague to make this woman keep that smelly hat at home, but I'm also tired of having to air the room out twice a day and eat my lunch in the teachers' breakroom. Marcy eats her lunch in there at the same time, and I'm exhausted with her nasty looks and grumbly attitude.

"Now that we have all of that out of the way, I wanted to speak with you about the fundraiser."

I smile and listen as she goes through a very impressive elevator pitch on raising money for a local event. I'm grateful enough that she leaves with a promise of no more raccoon hat, and no commitment from me to assist with whatever she has in mind for an ice cream social, and a smile on her face.

The rest of the day goes by slowly until the principal stops by near the end of the day, informing me that I've been here long enough to help with the after-school pickup line. I wanted to help since day one, but apparently it's a big deal, having the kids near traffic and all, that I needed to be vetted fully before being deemed responsible enough to supervise them outside of the classroom and in the fenced playground area at the back of the school.

I should be ashamed to be so excited for the end of the day. Well, maybe not ashamed for the day ending. I love my students, but everyone wants to get off work and have a little time to themselves.

My shame stems from hoping Kalen is the one picking Justin up this afternoon. Wanting to see the man is terrible because he's clearly married. I mean, he wasn't wearing a ring—another thing I shamefully checked for—when he was here earlier. I'll never admit out loud that I watched his butt the entire time he walked out of the classroom.

Back to his ring, or lack thereof... he wasn't wearing one, but I was told people around here don't get divorced. I think it was more of a warning than anything when Marcy just let loose that information one day in the breakroom. I mean, statistically, divorce happens to over forty percent of couples, and I doubt Lindell, Texas is immune to it, but that's not the point.

Kalen is one of my student's parent, and that makes him off-limits despite his good looks and admittedly charming failure at flirting.

Oh God.

If he's married and still flirting?

Jesus, what an asshole.

I keep this in mind, sneering at him as Justin climbs inside of his truck. I don't get close enough to speak with him because I'm still not allowed to be one of the loading assistants, but he frowns when he sees me. Literally, I watch the smile fall from his handsome face before I turn back around to calm Sammy down when he sees an old truck pull forward.

I need to get Kalen Alexander out of my head because it's never going to happen. He's a parent. He's a jerk. He's a horrible man.

Chapter 4

Kalen

"What did you do to that girl?" I ask, my eyes on the paperwork on the podium.

"Nothing," he grumbles. "She hates me for no good reason."

"Women don't hate people for no reason," I assure him. "You did something, Collins."

I look up at my younger cousin, a smirk on my face. This wouldn't be the first time the guy has angered a woman. It's a family trait. After what happened at the elementary school last week, I'd say the legacy continues.

"I swear," he hisses. "I've tried to talk to her a hundred times, and she just turns her nose up at me. Most days, she stares right through me as if I never opened my mouth."

"Immune to your charms?" I chuckle, feeling a little wounded myself. Damn McKenna Kaiser and her pretty eyes, perfect mouth, and sultry voice. "How does that make you feel?"

His eyes travel back to the very end of the first row in my classroom. Oakleigh Guthrie, a junior here at Lindell University, is focused on her notes, and I don't miss the fact that every other woman in the classroom has their sights set on us, or more specifically my cousin, Collins Alexander.

Many people don't know he's Linnie the Lemur, the small town university's infamous mascot, and that's by design. His contract—connected to his full-ride scholarship—with the school requires that his identity is kept a secret, a source of irritation for him because he wants everyone to know he's the guy in the costume that has had more viral online videos than can be counted.

"Move on from her then."

"I can't. She's—" His eyes scrape up her body from the no-nonsense Chucks on her feet to the pile of hair on top of her messy head. "She's perfect."

I shake my head.

"And she doesn't know you exist."

"You're one to talk," he says, shoving me in the shoulder.

I cock an eyebrow and glare at him. "You can't do that here. Everyone in this room just witnessed you shoving a teacher. I'm a freaking professional."

His grin grows at my growl, his eyes darting around the room. It's as if he's just now noticing the other twenty people or so in the room looking at him. He's no stranger to attention, and it's clear he doesn't normally pay it any mind.

"You're one to talk," he hisses, his head and voice lowered now that he realizes we're not the only two privy to this conversation.

"Don't know what you're talking about."

"I may be hot for Oakleigh, but you're hot for teacher."

Suddenly, the paperwork on the podium becomes insanely interesting. I should've known people were already talking. I wouldn't doubt that Marcy saw and heard my bumbling attempt to flirt with McKenna and spread it all over town. It would explain the looks I keep getting at Brew and Chew when I go in for my morning cup of coffee.

"Have you even spoken with her?" he prods.

"I have class, Mr. Alexander. Can you please take your seat so we can get started?"

With his back fully facing the classroom, he stares at me as if he's a barrier to the focused eyes in the room. "You haven't, have you, *Mr. Alexander*?"

I grind my teeth, not entirely annoyed with him, but getting there quickly. Getting shot down is one thing. Getting shot down and the entire town hearing about it is another.

"You see her every day," he reminds me.

I don't need the reminder. Picking up my nephew is now the highlight of my day. So, what if I'm a little tortured by his new teacher supervising the car pickup line?

"Do you get tongue tied at the sight of her? Does she make butterflies swim in your little belly?" he teases.

Yes and yes. More specifically, I stare straight ahead when I sense her looking in my direction because I've never put my foot in my mouth so quickly before.

"No," I lie.

"Yeah, right."

I want to grab him by his shirt collar when he turns to walk away, thinking he got the last word.

"At least she talks to me!" I say a little too loud to his back. I mean, she did during the parent/teacher conference, and that has to count for something, right? "That's more than you can say about, Oak—"

When I feel my cousin's crush snap her eyes up at me, I slam on the brakes.

Didn't I just tell that idiot I'm a professional?

That's the bad thing about teaching at my hometown college. I know half the people I'm tasked with teaching. They've heard the stories of how wild I was in high school and then again attending this very college. They know a litany of things no student should know about their instructors, especially if the instructor expects to be respected in his field.

Collins glares at me as he takes his seat in the fourth row back, but when Oakleigh flips her hair over her shoulder to start taking notes for class, he forgets all about me. If he thinks I'm going to keep emailing notes from class because he's too busy staring at her, he's wrong.

I shove thoughts of McKenna away as best I can and begin class. It'll only be a few more hours until I can pretend I don't see her outside of the school.

***

"He did it twice again yesterday," my sister Kristina says as she stirs macaroni and cheese on the stove.

My eyes turned to my nephew, Justin. "Seriously, dude?"

A five-year-old little boy just looks at me, a lost expression on his face, and shrugs his tiny shoulders.

"We talked about this, man. You can't be grabbing your junk on the playground at school."

"Maybe if you wouldn't—"

I turn to glare at my sister. "I don't grab my junk. That's something that Collins would do, not me."

"Collins doesn't come around very often. If he's acting like that at school, he gets it from you."

I turn my attention back to Justin. "Who have you seen grabbing their junk?"

My nephew, focused on the small pile of Legos in front of him, shrugs again.

"Are you listening to me? Don't do that sh-stuff anymore." I think I've grown out of dick grabbing as a response to something I didn't like in high school.

"Just because you have a crush on my teacher doesn't mean that I can act any differently at school."

My eyes narrow. "I do not have a crush on your teacher."

The little five-year-old scoffs, a sarcastic sound making my hackles go up. It's bad enough that I go to the Brew and Chew and get stared at now, but now I have to deal with this shit at home to?

Kristina laughs. "Really?"

"Don't even pretend you haven't heard about what happened at the parent/ teacher conference," I mutter.

"Oh, I heard, but it was because Ms. Kaiser called me."

"Called you?" I look around the room for my sister's phone. If that beauty called, then her phone number is now accessible.

"She didn't feel like you were paying attention. He can't keep getting into trouble in school, Kalen. I don't want my son to be *that kid* in class."

"He's not *that kid*," I argue. "He has a personality. You don't want him to be a drone."

"I went to the corner store and Marlene asked me if I'd gotten a handle on Justin's filthy mouth." She turns to glare at me.

It's my turn to shrug, but Kristina isn't going to give me the leeway we both give to Justin.

"What? He's sneaky. I can't help it if he's always lurking around, listening to adult conversations. He should be in trouble, not me."

"You should be more aware," she reminds me—a conversation we've had many times in the last two years that they've lived with me. "It's bad enough that—"

Her eyes dart to Justin who seems like he's fully concentrating on the Legos, but we both know better. Her voice becomes a low whisper that even I have trouble hearing.

"He's already the kid who doesn't have a dad. I don't want him to be alienated further."

Justin has a dad. I mean, obviously. Kristina at twenty-six years old didn't go to a sperm bank to be impregnated. According to the rumors that fly around town, that happy occurrence happened in the back seat of Kyle Lingram's Dodge Charger. The guy was always a douche growing up, and that didn't change the day Kristina told him he was going to be a father. It took the man less than a month to disappear from Lindell, and he hasn't been seen since.

"He does just fine," I remind her. "He's the most popular boy in his class."

I've witnessed this—all the other kids waiting for parents in the pickup line waving at him as he climbs in my truck.

"Aren't you going out?"

I cock an eyebrow. "Trying to get rid of me already?"

She does that hand on her hip thing, very similar to the way McKenna did it days ago in the school hallway, and it makes me wonder if this is something girls are taught early in life to display their annoyance.

I raise my hands in surrender, knowing a grumpy sister has the ability to make my life a living hell.

"I'm going." I shoot her a wink. "Don't wait up."

"Get it, Uncle Kalen." Looking over, I find Justin dancing like a fool, hip thrusts included.

I laugh of course, because it's hilarious to see my forty pound nephew swinging his hips around, but Kristina growls at him.

"Go get washed up for dinner," she tells him, exhaustion in her tone.

My laughter dies on my lips when I open the front door to find none other than McKenna Kaiser with her hand raised as if she was about to knock.

Play it cool, Kalen. This is your second chance.

"Funny seeing you here."

Not my best, but definitely not my worst.

I still scrunch my nose up, hating that this girl has the power to fluster me so badly.

"Mr. Alexander," she snips, but I don't miss the way her eyes trail over my bicep that flexes when I lean into the doorframe. I'm hoping for a casual approach, but when her eyes meet mine again, I just feel like an idiot.

"McKenna," I purr, but she doesn't grin with the way her name rolls off my tongue.

"I'm here to see, Kristina," she says, making it apparent she's ready to see the end of me.

I search her eyes. This girl isn't playing hard to get. I encounter that on occasion, women who spend too much time gossiping with others in town. They form an opinion of me quickly, but the charm and good looks eventually win them over.

God, even in my head I sound like a complete douchebag.

McKenna Kaiser isn't one of those women. I don't impress her at all. No games, no hint that I should try harder, just flat out leave me alone, I don't have time for you.

"She's in the kitchen," I mutter as I step to the side.

If she paused walking into the house, if she tilted her head the slightest fraction, I'd stick around and try my luck, but she doesn't. Getting shot down for a third time by this woman would be too much of a blow to my ego.

So, I close her inside, grumbling the entire way to my truck, and go about my night.

Chapter 5
McKenna

The Alexander house is tidy, but cleanliness was never one of my worries where little Justin is concerned. He's always in fresh clothes. He never shows up to class with his hair all over the place or remnants of breakfast on his face.

God, if I'm being truthful with myself, the entire reason I'm here just walked out the front door.

Did I plan to tell Justin's mother that her husband is a merciless flirt?

Are they still even married?

Why does any of it bother me to begin with?

I shouldn't be here.

But as I turn to leave, Kristina, Justin's mother, comes into the entryway. She grins at me. She looks tired, but I don't get a vibe that she's nervous that I'm here.

"Hi," I say, holding out my hand to shake hers. "I'm McKenna Kaiser. It's nice to finally meet you."

She shakes my hand. "Kristina Alexander. I'm honestly surprised we're just now meeting. Join me in the kitchen?"

My eyes dart around the house as I follow her into the equally tidy kitchen.

"I'm sorry I missed the parent/teacher meeting, but work is crazy right now."

"I'm glad you invited me over."

"May I get you something to drink? Sweet tea?"

"Sure, sweet tea is fine," I answer. I shift my weight back and forth on my feet, still not a hundred percent certain that I won't dart out of this house like someone lit me on fire.

"I know Justin is a handful, and I know I may sound like a hippie, but I just don't want to crush his spirit. He's going to have enough of that once he's older."

"He's an amazing kid. He's—"

"He's something else," Kristina says as she hands me a glass of iced tea. "But I think he means well most of the time."

"He's mischievous," I say with a smile, loving that the boy has a personality much bigger than his tiny frame. "He gets along well with all the kids at school."

"Is that teacher speak for he's a ringleader and is able to convince all the other students to do his bidding?"

I grin. There's no pulling wool over this momma's eyes.

"I think that's an accurate representation."

"He gets it from his father," she says with a sigh, taking her own glass of tea and settling in one of the dining room chairs. She waves me over and points to one of the others. I settle in although her last statement makes my skin tingle.

"Being manipulative?"

She tilts her head, and I realize what I asked. She may imply that her son is mischievous, but my focus was more on his dad and opinions I've formed of him. It's not the best word to describe a child.

"I mean—"

She chuckles. "I know what you meant. Justin will push any and all boundaries an adult will set, but I know he does well with consistency and routine."

"All the little boys in his class are the same way." I think back to each of my students. "Correction, all of them—even the girls—are that way. It's their age I think."

"So, he's not causing any more trouble than the next kid."

"No," I answer honestly. "He does it with a little more pizzazz than some of the others, but I'm being honest when I tell you that he's a joy to have in class. He's helpful and one of the few that doesn't jump on the bandwagon when another kid is found lacking by their peers. He defends the underdog and doesn't tolerate others being mean at all."

Translation—if Justin sees someone being picked on, he's quick to knock the bully on his ass, but I don't give her the dirty details. I've corrected the behavior when I see it, and he now knows that violence against a peer carries the same weight as the punishment for the bullies.

She gives me a weak smile, but I can see the relief on her face. "I'm doing my absolute best. I have a lot of help, but at the end of the day, being a single parent is hard. Much harder than I thought it was going to be."

So, they are separated.

"If I've learned anything, it's that people in town are always willing to help. It's a wonderful community."

She scoffs. "If by willing to help you mean nosy, then yes, they're willing to help."

I give her another smile for once wishing I wasn't Justin's teacher because I could see becoming friends with this woman.

We chat a little longer before I say my goodbyes, and when I walk out of her front door, I've convinced myself that Kalen Alexander is just a headache I don't want. It doesn't matter that he's separated from Kristina. If the man helps so little that she still feels like a single parent, then he's not the kind of guy I would be caught dead with.

***

Courtney was already at my place when I finished my visit with Kristina Alexander, and she didn't waste a moment turning me right back around and shoving me out the door.

"We're not staying in."

"There isn't any other place to go. Unless you're hungry. Are you hungry?"

"I googled the town while I was waiting and there's a bar."

"The Hairy Frog?"

"That's the one, and it's within walking distance."

"Everything is within walking distance," I mutter as she loops her arm through mine. "I haven't been there, but I'm sure it's filled with college students."

She tugs me closer, to the point I nearly stumble over my own feet.

"You mean legal men looking for a good time with a hot chick?"

"I mean students who probably aren't even old enough to drink," I correct.

"But legal," she says standing firm.

"I'm not hooking up with a college student," I mutter.

"We'll see."

We chat about mutual friends and about her desire to leave her job, but I know she'll never give it up. She lives for the chaos her boss creates, and it gives her a sense of purpose, something she's yearned for since her adopted mother passed away a couple of years ago. Courtney thrives in pandemonium, and her boss gives her that on a daily basis.

"Wow," my friend mumbles as we near the bar.

The place is so crowded that people are pouring out the front door. The music is so loud we can hear it from a block away. By the time we make it into the parking lot, we can feel the bass under our shoes. I'm getting a preemptive headache just thinking about going inside.

"Stop," Courtney says when I sigh a little too loudly. She spins me around with my back to the bar and glares at me. "We're going to have a great time. Since when are you such a stick in the mud?"

"I'm not," I argue, my brows knitting together. "I'm tired. I chase around a dozen five-year-olds all day. It's exhausting."

"All you need is a couple drinks and a long ride from a hot guy."

I don't bother arguing with her again when she spins us back around and ushers me toward the front door of The Hairy Frog.

I realize the place is much more spacious on the inside than it appears from outside, and as we walk deeper inside, it's nice to discover that the music isn't as loud as it seems either. The jukebox speakers are near the front door, so once we settle on the far end of the bar in two stools relinquished by two older southern gentleman with actual manners, we can actually speak with each other without yelling. Maybe the night is making a turn for the better.

We place our orders, the bartender not blinking an eye when Courtney orders two blended strawberry daiquiris.

"Tell me about the hot guy."

"Which hot guy?" I say, feigning interest in the straw sticking out of the top of my drink.

"Is there more than one in this town?" She gives me a knowing smile—one that tells me she's up for the challenge if I want to play dumb.

Not wanting to waste any more time on Kalen Alexander than I have to, I sigh. "He's no longer with his kid's mom, but I think he's a jerk."

"Jerks usually end up being very good lovers."

"I'm not—" I clamp my lips around my straw and suck down the entire contents of my drink, giving myself a brain freeze in the process. Even in conversation, Kalen is causing me grief.

"You're saying you haven't thought about him that way?"

I flag down the bartender, staying silent until after I order another drink, this one with a little extra kick. Courtney is like a dog with a bone, and I'm well aware the conversation won't end until she feels I've satisfied each one of her questions.

"Dating a student's parent is against school rules."

"It is not." She glares at me, but not shocked I have the audacity to lie to her. "The employee handbook is online, and that's not in there."

"It's one of the unspoken rules."

She rolls her eyes. "Is not. But he's hot, right?"

"You know he is." I said as much during a phone call when I was having a moment of weakness.

"How hot?"

I practically rip the new drink out of the bartender's hand when he offers it, but he simply smiles and nods as he steps away to help the next customer.

"So, freaking hot," I mutter.

"Then you know what you have to do." She bites the corner of her bottom lip, and I know that look. That look means trouble.

Probably more trouble than the man himself when I spot him across the bar. Of course, I don't say a word to him, but it's hard to look away when he spends the next twenty minutes surrounded by women vying for his attention.

He's more trouble than that look on my friend's face, and I'm glad I'm seeing him in action. It solidifies my decision to keep my distance from the man.

Chapter 6
Kalen

I growl at my best friend, pausing only to take a long pull from my beer.

It only makes him laugh harder.

"Remind me why we're friends again?"

Mac Hammer, my best friend since grade school, owns and operates a construction company here in town, and although he rarely uses his skills to build brand-new houses, the town is so old there's always someone needing a repair. The folks around here keep him busy, and he takes a lot of pride in his work. Having lived here all his life, he's very comfortable in town, and sometimes forgets that all of the people in the bar don't know him. The ones that do know that he can get a little wild and crazy, something I've tried to grow out of, or at least keep a tight lid on because there's no telling how many of the people in here tonight will attend one of my lectures at the university next week.

He grins around the mouth of his own beer. "Slim pickings."

There's probably more truth to that than he knows. Lindell is small, despite the atmosphere of The Hairy Frog. Being the only bar in town, it pulls not only the locals but students from the college as well. There are probably more people in here tonight than the population listed on the city limits sign.

It's Friday night, and that means the place is pulsing with music and people having a good time. The energy surrounding me would normally be enough to draw me in, make me smile and want to dance.

I've had the requisite three beers needed to get me on the dance floor, but my mood has been sour since leaving McKenna—sexy as hell, but unreasonable—Kaiser inside my house.

Mac thinks the entire situation is hilarious, but he's been bouncing between beer and shots tonight so everything is funny to him right now.

"So, she shot you down. Get over it."

"I'm over it," I hiss.

More laughter bubbles out of his throat. If I weren't unwilling to listen to him go on and on about my mood for the next month, I'd walk out of here. I mean, I can't go home because McKenna is there, but I could go sit and sulk at the local park until Sheriff Hodson threatens to call my mom as if I'm an unruly teen rather than a thirty-two-year-old man.

I really wish Cash Tucker, the Lindell Police Chief would hurry up and get someone hired so the Sherriff can go sit out on the highway rather than making patrols through town.

Speaking of Cash, it's no surprise to see Addalynn Tate sitting at the same table she sits at every night Cash works late. No one from out of town would believe they aren't together, but the company line is that they're just best friends. I think anyone but them can see how they look at the other, and it isn't with familiar friendly love.

"You know what I always say." He grins wide. "The best way to get over one woman is to get under another."

Mac pulls off his cowboy hat, swirling it around his head like he's riding a bronco. Several cheers from across the bar encourage him, but I look away when he starts smacking his jean-clad ass with his free hand. Idiots encouraging idiots.

"So why don't you try that?"

"Can't I enjoy my beer in peace?"

"Or," he waggles his eyes brows comically, "you could go see what that fine specimen at the bar is drinking and offer to buy her another."

I shake my head, not even bothering to look in the direction he's indicating. There's too great of a chance that whomever he's pointing at is a college student. Lindell is already a small pond, and one I refuse to go fishing in. I'm not taking the chance that I end up getting lucky with a woman only for her to direct me to the damn college dorms at the end of the night when I take her home. I like my job and hooking up with a student is the quickest way to get a foot in my ass.

We may be less than an hour away from Austin, but no night of fun is worth that daily drive.

"Look," he urges, physically taking my head in his hands and turning it in the direction of the bar.

And God, do I look, because it's not a college student standing at the bar with a wide grin, her perfect lips circling the straw sticking out of her fruity drink. It's McKenna. Her long blonde hair shines in the soft overhead lighting as she talks with another women I've never seen around town.

"See?" Mac prods. "Now go buy her a drink. Twenty bucks says you can get her in your truck in less than an hour."

I growl, the sound rumbling from deep in my chest. "Don't."

The single word means don't objectify her. Don't imply that she's easy. Don't look at her. Just… *don't*.

"Noooo," he hisses, his eyes darting between me and the gorgeous woman at the bar. He must not be drinking at the same rate as me because he has caught on way too quickly for my taste. "That's her?"

I don't justify his question with an answer. I simply turn my beer up to my mouth. My skin feels like it's on fire with her being so close.

"Shit, man. Now I see what the fuss is all about." I turn to face him, forcing him to stand on his tiptoes to see over my shoulder. "She's hot as hell. How many times have you imagined gripping a handful of that hair and—"

I shove him back before he gets too far into the hip thrusts very similar to what Justin was doing earlier tonight.

"You need to stop. Maybe act your age instead of five."

"But she likes five-year-olds," he says with a laugh, taking enough steps backward so I can't reach him when he starts humping the air again.

It takes the beer in my hand and the next one before I've finally convinced myself that approaching her for a third time is the best idea ever, but by the time I've made my decision, we've been surrounded by friends.

"I like it," I answer Beth when she asks me about my job at the college.

She frowns when I take a step back to keep her from putting her hand back on my arm. Most would say it's an innocent touch, but I have to wonder if she's trying for a repeat of last summer, but the woman told everyone I was her fiancé after a drunken make-out session at the park.

Thankfully, Sheriff Hodson prevented that from going any further, and we haven't really spoken since I confronted her when my mother demanded I come visit to select between a variety of *Save the Date* cards.

Beth went as far as registering for wedding gifts at The Devil's Lettuce, the only gift/herbal remedy shop in town. Hippie Jones wasn't very happy when I went in to cancel the registry. Apparently, you can never have too many "water pipes"—AKA bongs, because marijuana isn't legal in Texas.

I frown, looking over at Joy.

If I've ever been heartbroken, she would be the only one able to claim that achievement. Joy and I dated freshman and sophomore year at Lindell University where we both attended. She set her sights on an Oklahoma transplant, and as the saying goes in a small town, you don't lose your girlfriend, you lose your turn.

I lost my *turn* with Joy to—"Hey, man."

I shake Joy's husband's hand. It's very civil and mature, but he pulls her close to his side as if he finds the need to stake his claim over her.

Conversations continue, another beer is consumed, and I know I need to go make my move on McKenna. Maybe she's been standoffish because she was in work mode both times I've seen her. Having kept my eyes on her for most of the night, I know she's had a few drinks. The soft lights above her head do nothing to hide the heat on her cheeks from the alcohol.

I'm not into drunk girls. I'm not the type of man that lays in wait while women get drunk, then pounce. That shit's creepy.

I wouldn't give Mac the satisfaction of admitting it out loud, but I have in fact pictured McKenna and myself in many compromising situations, including one very detailed circumstance involving the plastic ruler I noted on her desk during the parent/teacher conference from hell.

That being said, I don't want to take her home... *tonight*.

There isn't a single part of my anatomy that looks at her and thinks a one-and-done is the right thing to do.

Hell, in my dream the other night, I spent what felt like years trying to wife the woman. It wasn't until Dream McKenna pushed me off a cliff while I was on one knee proposing at the Grand Canyon that I finally startled awake.

I just want to talk to her. I want one of those pretty smiles angled in my direction instead of flat lips and darting eyes as if she's planning her escape route.

"I think you missed the cutoff," Mac says when my eyes focus on McKenna.

I turn my beer up and drain it, shaking my head to disagree with him.

"Seriously, man." His alcohol-heavy words are a warning. "You go over there now, and she'll never speak to you again."

"It'll be fine," I assure him, pressing my empty bottle into his hand before grabbing a fresh one from the table in front of us. "She's so freaking pretty."

"You're going to crash and burn."

"Nonsense. I've got this." I clap him twice on the shoulder as I walk away, my sights homed in on the prettiest girl in the bar.

I didn't say bye to those that gathered around us, but I can't concentrate on the people from my past. I'm looking toward the future, looking at the gorgeous blonde with vibrant green eyes.

When she notices me approaching her, a vibrant smile spreads across her face, and I realize just how easy she's going to make this for me. I was right. She just needed a different atmosphere and time to loosen up.

My smile grows wider.

Then she frowns, as if she caught herself grinning, and changed her mind.

It's a warning bell, an alarm taking over the music slipping into the bar from the jukebox, but I'm two beers past being able to care about reading social cues.

I urge myself to act casual while part of my brain is insisting on a retreat as I lift my beer to my lips, but someone bumps into me. Time slows to a crawl as I watch my full beer slip from my hand. I wince when it hits the floor but smile triumphantly when it doesn't shatter. It tells me the world hasn't completely gone to shit, but then the damn thing spins like a top, foamy beer spraying out in a wide arcing circle, splashing not only everyone in a four-foot radius but getting all over McKenna's feet as well.

Has she been wearing those sexy ass boots all night?

Slowly, my eyes trail up her legs, past the top of her boots to the bare skin of her legs before meeting the hem of her dress. Jesus, what is it about a woman in boots and a dress that makes my heart stop?

The neckline dips between her breasts, just the faintest hint of cleavage on display, and by the time I make it to her frowning face, my mouth is hanging open because that's how horndogs pant, wide open mouth with tongue lolled out to the side.

She's absolutely stunning—*and angry.*

"Hey," I say as I get within hearing distance.

"You ruined my boots."

"Come back to my place, and I'll clean them for you." I say most of that without slurring, so I'm going to call it a win.

Her friend chuckles beside her, but I only have eyes for

McKenna.

"You were right. He's hot as hell." My ears perk up at her friend's comment.

I smirk at McKenna, letting her know I'm now aware she's been talking about me.

"He's an idiot," my girl snaps.

Her fingers trailing down the condensation on her drink shouldn't cause a physical reaction in my jeans, so I'm going to blame the alcohol on the throb settling there.

"Can we go somewhere and chat?" I bite my lower lip because it's worked for me in the past.

Her eyes dart to my mouth, but from the weirded-out look on her face, I must be doing it wrong.

"And pull you away from your harem of women?" She looks past me, no doubt catching evil eyes from Beth if she's still over there.

By noon tomorrow, I have no doubt Beth will have been able to convince some townsfolk that I'm openly cheating on her. The girl lives in a different world than everyone else.

"I don't have a harem," I tell her, trying to lean on the bar with my elbow and nearly falling on my ass. I recover and stand awkwardly in front of her. "But I am looking for my queen."

"Oh God," her friend mutters. "Are all the guys around here this cheesy?"

"Are you ready to go?" McKenna asks, acting as if I'm not standing right in front of her.

"And miss the entertainment?" Her friend scoffs. "I know you're playing hard to get, but if you spend too much time turning him down, I think I'm going to step in."

"Hard to get?" My smile is back.

"I never said that!" She glares at her friend, and I want to see how she's reacting, but I can't seem to pull my gaze from the beauty in front of me.

Some weird girl conversation goes on between the two of them with simple looks, and I'm lost. I wouldn't be able to understand this language fully sober, so it's impossible now.

"We're leaving," McKenna snaps as she stands from the bar stool. She steps around me, grabbing at her friend. "Let's go."

"What?" her friend whines as she tries to polish off her drink before McKenna pulls the straw from her mouth.

"I'm never telling you anything again."

"Seriously? He's drunk. He won't remember a damn thing in the morning."

I watch them leave the bar with a smile on my face.

In case you are wondering, her friend is wrong. I have an amazing memory. It's how I got through grad school with little effort.

Chapter 7
McKenna

Since I didn't have enough to drink last night to give me a hangover, I'm blaming the headache I woke with this morning on stress. I fully blame Kalen Alexander even though it was less than ten minutes of interaction with him.

That ten minutes led to a restless night's sleep and dreams so vivid I'll never speak of them to a soul.

Who cares if dream me was open to his suggestions?

Awake me would never go there.

"How did you sleep?" I ask Courtney as she drags herself into the kitchen fifteen minutes after me.

"Not well," she mutters as she makes a beeline to the pot of coffee on the counter. "Kevin called at midnight, and I didn't get done with work until after three."

She rubs at her eyes with the back of her hands.

"Thought you were on vacation?" I tilt my own coffee mug to my lips so she can't see the sneer on my face.

We've had more than one conversation about how her boss abuses her time. She won't listen, and although she hasn't said as much, I think she's in some sort of relationship with him, which only makes things more complicated.

"It was important."

It always is. "I think you need to try one of the omelets from the Brew and Chew."

Courtney laughs, just like she's done every time I mention the name of the businesses around here, but she's too tired for full effort.

"They have espresso."

Courtney glares at me as if I've just insulted her.

"There's espresso in this town and we're here drinking this?" She holds up her cup, disgusted like I've offered her sludge instead of coffee made from beans I special order online.

"The town is pretty laid back," I tell her, my eyes skating down her t-shirt and sleep shorts. "But you may need to put on a little more clothes."

She grumbles about the town needing a delivery service, but I ignore her. I'm much more active since moving to Lindell simply because many of the conveniences I thought I couldn't live without aren't in town. I miss rushing through a fast-food drive-thru, but I also can admit how much better I feel with increased movement and less junk in my diet.

Despite—or maybe because—Courtney needs coffee, it still takes her nearly an hour to get ready, but when she reemerges, she's decked out, full makeup and her hair shines like a new penny. I look down at the sweats and loose t-shirt I'm wearing, but I refuse to change. It's the Brew and Chew not a dinner date at the top of the Reunion Tower in Dallas. I have no one to impress, and my effort in my appearance speaks that loud and clear. People are right when they say they've never seen two pretty best friends.

Courtney must be picking her battles because she doesn't say anything to me as we walk out of my duplex and head in the direction of the diner.

"I'm sleeping with Kevin," Courtney blurts after the waitress drops off our coffees.

"Okay," I begin because I really don't know what else to say.

She knows it can't end well. She knows it's a bad idea.

She doesn't need to hear me repeat that, so I don't know what else to give her.

"Do you love him?"

"It's not about love," she says, but when she looks out the window, I can tell that she's gone for the guy. The unhappy look means he doesn't feel the same way. Unrequited love sucks. At least, that's what I hear because I don't think I've ever been in love before.

She brought the subject up, but just as quickly she changes it.

"Tell me more about this guy from last night."

I shake my head. "If you're not talking about your love life, I'm not talking about mine."

She grins, her eyes bright and as full of mischief as I've ever seen.

"What?" I hiss, unsure if I should look over my shoulder. I swear if Kalen is in this diner, I'll get up and walk out, forcing her to pay for our coffees and uneaten breakfast.

"I've never seen you so adamant about not wanting to talk about a guy before."

"And yet it still hasn't deterred you," I mutter.

"He's hot. Not like the best-looking in town, but one of the better looking guys I've ever seen. He's Hollywood hot, not hometown sweetheart hot."

"I'm painfully aware of how good looking the man is."

"Then you should—"

"This is a small town. Dating him—"

"I never said anything about dating him."

"Doing *anything* with Kalen Alexander would only complicate things."

What I don't say is that as much as I questioned my decision to move here, this town is slowly growing on me. I can see myself making a life here but hooking up with one of my student's parents would be a mistake of epic proportions. Even a little fun between the two of us would spread like wildfire in this town.

"What about that guy?"

I turn slightly to see where she's pointing and huff a laugh. It isn't one of the Tate brothers as I feared, but Abraham Fisher.

"That's the mayor," I whisper when I turn back around.

"Why the lowered voice?" she asks, leaning in just like Mrs. Hinkle did last week during the parent/teacher conference. I laugh a little, realizing gossip is everyone's favorite subject in school.

"Did you see him smile?"

"Huge teeth," Courtney confirms.

"Fake teeth," I say. "Rumor has it he was caught in bed with another man's woman."

"And the guy knocked his teeth out?"

I nod. "I know there's more to the story, but I've only picked up bits and pieces. From what I understand, the dentist in town was the cheating woman's husband. Old Abe over there threatened to file charges if his teeth weren't fixed. I don't know if the dentist made them that big on purpose or if the man originally had big teeth."

Courtney giggles. "Really? Debauchery in a small town, huh? I freaking love it. After we eat, I want to meet the hippie."

Hippie Jones easily convinces Courtney to spend a pretty penny in his store, and I walk out feeling better about myself knowing I'm not the only one he's able to sell Arizona-based oceanfront property to. The man is devious, and he does it all with a smile on his face.

"Do you want me to carry that?" Courtney asks when I shift my shopping bag from one hand to the other.

"I didn't know he kept track of what I've already purchased. I was certain I'd be able to buy another one of those small green ones, but he knew I already had one. Now I'm stuck buying the bigger ones. Glass is heavy."

She laughs, her arm going through my free arm as we walk toward That's Another Story.

"Are there going to be any weirdos at the bookstore?"

"Never know," I answer with a shrug. "We haven't run into the Tate brothers, so there's still a good chance of meeting them."

I see them everywhere, and since that one interaction in the diner, I go the other way if I see their truck. They ruined my craving for pizza the other night when I saw them parked outside of Knead Pizza. I had to settle for a frozen one from the corner store, but at least Marlene hooked me up with my favorite candy bars.

"The dating duo?" Courtney asks, smiling wide when I answer in the affirmative. "I hope we do. I still think you're lying about those guys.

There's no way men from such a small town only date the same woman."

Our spirits are light as we enter That's Another Story.

"Hey, McKenna. I was going to call you."

"My books are in?" I'm near giddy when Oakleigh guides me to the front counter. "They arrived late yesterday evening."

Courtney heads off to find a book to read on her flight home tomorrow, and I shuffle through the books I bought for my classroom. The ones left behind by Mrs. Eaton were old and worn, and there are so many new titles I feel like the kids at school would enjoy. I went a little overboard in ordering, but each and every one will be read to my students by the end of the school year, and if Mrs. Eaton comes back, and I'm not offered another classroom, I'll leave them behind for the next group of kindergarteners to enjoy.

"How's school going?" I ask Oakleigh, knowing from my multiple visits before that she's a full-time college student at Lindell University.

"It's fine," she huffs.

"You sure?" She nods. "But that guy is still bothering you?"

"The guys from this town are relentless. Collins is no different. He thinks he's God's gift to women and is shocked that I have no interest in him."

I nod, knowing another man exactly like that. My boots will reek of beer for the foreseeable future because of a man exactly like that.

"He'll go away eventually," I assure her as I set my bag from The Devil's Lettuce on the floor at my feet and pull out my wallet.

"It would be easier if he wasn't so cute."

"Maybe going out with him wouldn't be so bad," I say, feeling like Courtney in her pursuit to convince me that hooking up with Kalen is a good idea. I regret the words immediately.

"I know his type, and I'm not interested in being anyone's bedpost notch."

I nod in understanding. "Well, stay strong then."

I wave at Sage, the owner of the bookstore as she shuffles past with her arms full of new release copies she's showcasing near the front of the store.

"Hey, McKenna."

I give her a smile before turning my attention to Courtney as she steps up to the register.

She decides on a thriller for her plane ride back, and it isn't long until we're once again walking down the street arm in arm, chatting about anything and everything. Thankfully, she seems to have given up on discussing our love lives.

But when she's gone the next day, it only takes a few hours for my mind to drift back to him. There has to be something in the water in this tiny town because I've never not been able to get my mind off someone once I decide to do so.

Chapter 8
Kalen

I'm nervous.

I'm never nervous.

Well, I was nervous once before in life, but I don't know anyone going in for their first physical knowing a doctor is going to squeeze their nuts while asking them to cough that doesn't get a little nervous. Add in the fact that it was a woman, and my hands were trembling while I chanted *don't get hard, don't get hard* over and over in my head. Also ignore the fact that Dr. Millway was pushing sixty at the time. When a teenage boy's nuts get touched by someone other than himself for the very first time, things just happen.

I clear my throat as I climb out of my truck, but even shaking my hands down at my sides doesn't ease my jitters.

I know now isn't a good time to speak with Ms. Kaiser, but while she stands outside with her class waiting for parents to pick the little devils up, I know she can't walk away and leave them alone.

It provides the perfect opportunity for me to apologize for my behavior Saturday night.

Yeah, Mom called and demanded I beg for forgiveness from the pretty teacher, but I also felt bad. Mostly I felt the urge to track her down in town on Sunday but asking around would only bring more scrutiny and I've gotten enough already where she's concerned. The woman hasn't stuck around for longer than a five-minute conversation and I got wind that's there's already a pool going on as to how long it will take for her to either kick me in the sac or fall in love with me. Sadly, my best friend, Mac, is on *team kick him in the nuts*, and the jerk doubled down after I sprayed her with beer.

McKenna is singing a calm-down song, something about having patience when I walk up. And her voice is… awful. It's a cross between screeching and a braying donkey, but it only endears me to her more. It's good to know she's not perfect in all things.

Her mouth snaps shut when she notices me walking toward her, and her hand shoots out when Justin stands to run to me. I'm glad she's still aware of everything going on around. I wish I could say the same thing because a horn blares as I watch her, pulling my attention and making me realize I literally just walked into traffic while my eyes were glued to the delicate features of her face.

I give the car a quick wave of apology only to find Old Man Hinkle shaking a finger at me. Geez, this could've ended badly. I know for a fact the man can't see. I've caught him more than once carrying on a one-sided conversation with the elm tree outside of the post office.

Justin is glaring at me as I walk closer, as if it's my fault his teacher won't let him play in traffic.

"Hey, Freddie," my nephew says as I reach the two of them. He tilts his head up to look at McKenna. "Can we go now?"

"Just a second, buddy," I tell him before turning to McKenna. "Can we talk?"

"I'm working." Her cheeks rise, the fake smile on her face making it very clear that she doesn't suffer fools, and she thinks I'm the biggest one she's ever met.

"I wanted to apologize for my behavior Saturday night."

She swallows, her eyes trying to look past me, but I catch interest there as her gaze falls on my mouth before darting away. I clench my fingers tightly in a fist to keep from pumping my arm up and down in victory. She's interested, and I'd know that for sure even if I hadn't overheard her friend mention it at the bar a couple of nights ago.

"I don't normally get that—" She clears her throat to keep me from going into detail around such delicate ears. When I look over, I find a dozen little faces looking up at the two of us. "I feel like we need to start over. Is that—"

"Hellooo?" I look down at Justin, trying to give him a look that tells him I may be making progress with this pretty girl and he needs to chill, but he's five, and the dude sucks at reading social cues. "Ready, Freddie?"

"Yeah, I'm—" I look back up at her. "Just, sorry. I hope it doesn't reflect poorly—"

"Freddie!" Geez, read the room, kid.

"I better go. I'm going to be at the Easter egg hunt on Sunday. I hope to see you there."

"Have a good day," she says as she waves a little girl forward because her mother is pulling up in the pickup lane.

I've been thoroughly dismissed.

It may not be the excited interaction I was hoping for, but at least she didn't walk away from me this time. I call that progress, folks.

Justin is quiet the entire walk back to the truck, and that makes me extremely suspicious.

He keeps his eyes straight ahead regardless of the times I glance at him in the rearview mirror.

"What did you do?"

He swallows, his little throat working, but he still won't make eye contact with me.

"Do I even want to know?" That question gets a slight eyebrow raise but nothing else. "Is this something that's going to upset your mother?"

His eyes dart away. "It's not a big deal."

Translation—it's a very big deal and I'm screwed.

"Do you want to work through it now, or do you want to just deal with it with your mom?"

He thinks it over for a while, and just when I think he's going to be the stubborn little boy we all know and love, he opens his mouth. "It wasn't even a big fire."

"What?" I snap, thankful I'm pulling into the driveway. "You started a fire at school?"

He snaps his head in my direction. "This is your fault, not mine."

"M-Mine? How do you figure that?"

"You're—" He jabs his little pointer finger in my direction. "You're the one who gave me the magic set for Christmas."

I huff. This isn't my fault. Kristina got that and put my name on it. I suck at buying gifts, and the year before, he wasn't very impressed with the math flash cards I got him, despite the kit having addition, subtraction, *and* multiplication. It came in a shiny tin box with a lock to keep them safe. It was a really cool gift, and I'm getting off topic. Suffice it to say, my nephew won't be a math nerd like I am. I wish I could say I haven't lost sleep over it but...

I digress.

"Hold on. That magic kit didn't have anything that would catch fire. The most dangerous thing in the kit was that spring-loaded bunny that pops out of the hat. Now that thing nearly caught me in the eye. Do you remember when—"

"Can you focus?" he snaps. "Mom's going to hang me by my toenails!"

"What and how did you catch something on fire?"

"A roll of toilet paper in the bathroom."

"And how does this have anything to do with the magic kit?" I prod.

"The kit inspired me. Have you ever seen a real magic show without puffs of smoke? I used the lighter *you* left near the grill out back. You should really put things back where they belong. They're dangerous for kids my age."

I close my eyes, taking a deep breath through my nose. When I open them again, this child is looking at me like the entire thing is my fault, and that Kristina is going to be hanging me up by my toenails.

"So, it's my fault you got the lighter?" He nods. "And my fault you smuggled it to school and lit a roll of toilet paper on fire."

"And Mom is going to be so mad at you."

I climb out of my truck, rolling my eyes the entire time. This kid. If he weren't the spitting image of me when I was his age, I'd have more to say.

"Did your teacher call your mother?"

He shakes his head as he drags his backpack along the ground behind him. "She said she felt bad for Mom since she had to deal with you all the time. She wrote a note and put it in my backpack."

I scoop up the backpack and go digging.

"Really?" I snap, holding up one of my expensive watches. "You took this, too?"

"The girls in second grade like shiny things. Who am I to deprive them?"

"No more hanging out with Mac." Those words could've come right from my best friend's mouth. "And my electric razor? How long have you had this? I had to buy another one when this went missing!"

He shrugs as he climbs the front porch steps.

"There's no note in your backpack, Justin. What did you do with it?"

He grins, a maniacal look that would make me consider having him tested for psychopathy if I hadn't witnessed him crying over an animated movie last week.

"I tore it into tiny pieces and ate it."

Chapter 9
McKenna

Flustered, I sit in my car after seeing my last student climb into his mother's car.

The one time I actually needed to talk to Kalen, and my head wouldn't work right. I can imagine the sly grin he'd get on his face if he ever found out he distracted me just by walking up to me outside of school.

I practiced what I was going to say to him time and time again after catching the four boys in the bathroom around a smoldering roll of toilet paper.

Justin didn't have the lighter. He wasn't the one to light the roll. That task was left up to Sammy. He was the only one in the group with hands big enough to strike the damn thing, but Justin was proud when he confessed that it was his idea, as if he was the first person on earth to create fire. The other three scrambled when I shoved open the restroom door. Justin just beamed up at me and pointed.

"Grab some marshmallows, Ms. K! We can make s'mores!"

It was a tiny fire, and it took a lot not to laugh at the pride in his eyes.

The principal wasn't impressed, but she also insisted that notes home were the best action instead of calling parents.

"They're five not hardcore felons, McKenna. I'm sure they're sorry. Let's move on."

She made me feel like I was ready to get the police involved, but I get the feeling that boys around here cause tons of trouble for school staff and their parents. I know someone would've gotten suspended if they did that in my kindergarten class. It was true when I told Courtney that the people around here are much more laid back. I don't know if that's a good thing or detrimental to these kids later in life.

Mondays are always long and exhausting. The kids are coming

back from a weekend of running around and free energy and it's up to the teachers to calm them enough to get them back in the mindset to learn. Tomorrow would be better.

But that doesn't solve my problem about today. I just want to go home, eat and crash, but I didn't go grocery shopping because I didn't want to spend my limited time with Courtney doing menial things. So, my fridge is bare bones.

The Tate brothers' truck isn't parked outside of the Brew and Chew when I drive past, and I go ahead and pull in.

Maybe a quick dinner is just what I need to get rid of the Monday blues.

Since it's still between normal lunch and dinner hours, the diner is fairly empty. I wave to an older couple who always seem to be here as I take a seat at a booth in the back. If I had a hat and sunglasses, I'd be wearing them but in this town, I imagine that would stand out. Firstly, I've never seen anyone wear a hat inside any of the stores around here. That's a respect thing. Secondly, my wild blonde hair is like a beacon.

"What can I get you to drink, sweetie?" I grin up at Ruth. She's the owner at the Brew and Chew and is always scurrying around to help with tables. I hope to have half her energy when I'm her age.

"Just a water today, Ruth. Any specials?"

Ruth doesn't miss a beat telling me about the salad of the day and the chicken and dumplings—her memaw's recipe—and I decide to get a half serving of each because I couldn't pick between the two.

The water is delivered quickly, and the food not very long after. I'm moaning and groaning, mouth full of delicious flavors, wishing I could get memaw's recipe when a shadow falls over the table. I finish chewing before looking up, but then I'm startled when I see a woman beaming down at me instead of the Tate brothers.

"Hi," I say with genuine enthusiasm.

"McKenna Kaiser?" the smiling woman asks.

I nod, wiping my hand on my paper napkin before holding it out to her.

"I'm Mrs. Rebecca Shears. I wanted to welcome you to town." She grips my hand between both of her palms like my own granny used to do, and it automatically makes me feel right at home. Wrinkles form at the corners of her mouth and eyes, and it's easy to see they're there because she's spent a lifetime laughing, smiling, and enjoying her life.

"Please join me." I wave a hand to the other side of my booth.

"The chicken and dumplings?"

"Amazing," I say, a little put out that I have company and really want to dive back in.

"Please." She points to my bowl as if she can read my mind.

"Do I look that hungry?"

"You were mumbling its praises when I walked up. I felt bad for interrupting."

I chuckle but do as she insists, scooping up another heaping spoonful and shoveling it into my mouth.

"She only makes it on Monday, so keep that in mind."

"Such a shame. I wonder if it reheats well."

Mrs. Shears grins again. "It does, but she won't let you carry any of it out of here. She's afraid someone is going to analyze it and copy the recipe."

I cock an eyebrow. "Really?"

I cover my mouth, embarrassed that I just asked that with a mouthful of dumplings.

Mrs. Shears nods. "She's an amazing cook, but also a little nuts."

I nearly choke on my food, laughter bubbling out of my throat when she circles her pointer finger near her temple. I haven't met a completely sane person in this town yet, and since I'm falling in love with Lindell, I guess that means there's a little crazy in me as well.

"I know this is forward, but are you dating anyone?"

My spoon clatters into my bowl, but I don't look down at the soup I feel splatter on my shirt. I work with small kids all day. It wouldn't be the first thing to mark my clothes today.

"I'm sorry?"

"Dating? Do you have a boyfriend? A girlfriend? A friend with benefits?"

My eyes widen. Are they that progressive around here that they wouldn't bat an eye at a lesbian or someone sexually free enough to have a no-strings attached sexual relationship?

"No," I answer honestly because I'm too taken aback by such a direct question.

"So, you're not in a relationship?" I shake my head. "I think you'd be perfect for my son."

And the full truth comes out. She may be here to welcome me to town, but that's not her sole purpose of approaching me.

I sweep my eyes over her face, wondering if it's familiar. Does she have the same eyes as the Tate brothers? I'm not a hundred percent certain that she doesn't.

"I'm not looking to date anyone," I answer, only feeling mild relief that her last name isn't Alexander.

She gives me a soft smile. "He's an amazing man."

"I'm sure he's wonderful." I drop my eyes back to my chicken and dumplings and work on spooning up another bite.

"He's a complete gentleman." Definitely not Kalen's mother then, and that knowledge gives this man she speaks of more appeal than she'll ever know. "He's educated and has a good job. Never been married. No kids."

He's sounding better and better.

"He sounds wonderful."

"He really is." Her eyes are bright and happy, and seeing her smile makes me smile, and then I have to wonder if she's Hippie Jones' mother because he's just as easily able to convince me to buy things I don't need. "I can give you my phone number if you change your mind. Town can get kind of dull when you don't know anyone. Maybe he can show you around."

Am I really fixing to exchange phone numbers with this woman? How many relationships start with meddling women? Probably more than anyone realizes.

"That sounds like a perfect idea."

She pulls a business card from her little purse, and I look down at it in confusion.

"Sisters of Liberty?"

"I'm the president," she beams. "We're responsible for many of the fundraisers in town. May I have your number, dear?"

Wow. This woman is good.

"In case I need help with a fundraiser."

So very good.

I recite my phone number, too flustered to even give her the wrong one, the one I used when I would go out when I lived in Dallas.

She grins again before standing, wishing me a good evening, and disappearing out of the diner.

I'm left with a business card in my hand and a sinking feeling that I was just somehow bamboozled.

But then, I start eating again, and all thoughts of anything but this divine food disappears from my mind.

Chapter 10

Kalen

"This again?" I ask Collins as he stares longingly across the park.

Oakleigh is grinning down at a couple of kids as they talk animatedly about a book she's holding. Her smile is huge, and it's clear she's in her element.

"Get off my back, man," my cousin snaps. "Don't you see how pretty she is?"

She's very pretty. I'd say even gorgeous if I were into younger women. It's easy to see why my cousin is so enthralled. I won't tell him that despite his popularity that he's way out of his league with her. He'll find out soon enough on his own.

"So, go talk to her." If only I could take my own advice. I've seen McKenna no less than half a dozen times since arriving for the town's Easter festivities, and I haven't approached her. "I didn't know she worked at That's Another Story."

"She just started a couple of weeks ago," he muttered, his eyes glued to her like a lovesick fool.

"And you know that how? Are you stalking her?"

"Her best friend mentioned it."

"And you just happened to strike up a conversation with Kinsley Nash."

He turns his head to glare at me. "Why do you know who her best friend is, Kalen?"

I swear his chest puffs up in an effort to look more intimidating. Does he really think I'm interested in a college student?

"Really? I'm not going after your girl, and honestly, I find it sad that I know who's friends with who. This town is too small." I'm not really complaining. The size of the town has only helped me where McKenna is concerned.

But really, why haven't I thought about going to McKenna's best friend to try to get an in with the woman? My cousin may be ignorant most days, but this is genius.

My eyes dart all over the park, looking for the brunette I remember seeing her with at the bar.

"—and we just started talking. She mentioned—hey are you even listening to me?"

"What?" Man, he's worse than Justin when he needs attention.

"I ran into Kinsley in line in the cafeteria. She said her calendar cleared up because Oakleigh was working part time at the bookstore."

"Dude." I angle my head. "The girl was flirting with you."

"She won't even look at me unless I'm Lenny."

"Not Oakleigh you idiot, Kinsley."

"She wasn't," he argues.

"Do you know anything about women?" He frowns as if he really has to think about it. "A woman doesn't tell you she has an open calendar unless she's wanting you to fill it."

"But I like Oakleigh."

"Jesus, dude, really? You don't have to date Kinsley because she flirted. And I know what that look means. You can *not* tell Oakleigh that you're Lenny."

"She might talk to me if she knew."

"If she knew, you'd be in breach of your contract with the school, and if you lose your scholarship, you're out."

"It may be worth it. There are lots of colleges in Austin."

"Any that Oakleigh go to?" He frowns. "Exactly. You're just going to have to woo the girl the old-fashioned way."

"With like goats and stuff?"

"What?" I huff a laugh, because seriously, we aren't but nine years apart and I feel like he's talking a different language.

"A dowry."

This idiot. "Dowries are paid by the woman's family, you idiot. I mean the old-fashioned way like smiling, flirting, putting yourself in her path. Talking to her. That sort of thing."

"Sounds like a lot of work."

"Most girls worth fighting for are," I mutter, my eyes landing on McKenna as she walks across the park.

I shove Collins away with one final push toward the table set up by the local bookstore and smile as she approaches.

She has a soft smile on her face, but I think it's for Justin's benefit since he seems hell-bent to drag her all the way over here.

"Ms. Kaiser," I say when she's close.

The wind ruffles her hair, and I take a deep breath. She smells like... goats? Or is Collins mention of a dowry somehow stuck in my head?

"What's that—" My nose scrunches, and once again she doesn't look impressed. "Hey, buddy. Where's your mom?"

McKenna looks around nervously, releasing Justin's hand and taking a step back.

"She's getting lemonade and cookies, but the guy at the stand keeps asking her to go to dinner. The poor fool can't take a hint." Justin shakes his head, and I swear he's a parrot, mimicking everything he hears because Kristina said that very same thing about the guy at Knead Pizza last week. The thing is my sister doesn't understand men who have no problem dating a single mother, and that's on the damage her ex did to her.

"I'm going to..." McKenna hitches a thumb over her shoulder, suddenly becoming uneasy. "I just wanted to make sure he didn't get lost."

"Who?" I ask.

"Justin." She points to him as he darts away with a couple of friends from school. "Shouldn't you go after him?"

"He'll be fine," I assure her. She's new to town, but everyone here—well, mostly everyone—pays close attention to everyone, including the kids. Not only do they do it to keep them safe in our wonderful, small town, but they're always looking for a reason to gossip. If Justin so much as picks his nose, we'll hear about it before dinnertime.

"Have you convinced her to go out on a date with you yet?"

Did I mention how annoying sisters are?

"We weren't—that's not what we were doing. I was—" McKenna rakes a flustered hand over the top of her head and it suddenly hits me why she's been distant. Okay, that's a cocky thought, and probably not the only reason since I seem to muck every conversation with her up, but this woman thinks Kristina and I are in a relationship.

After shuddering at the mere thought of dating my sister—our town is small, but we aren't backwoods small—I can't stop the grin that spreads across my face.

"Keep giving me shit, and I'll tell Mom about the time you snuck out to go skinny dipping with the Tate brothers." I angle my head in the direction of the two guys who haven't changed much since high school. Ronnie is picking corn out of his teeth with a meaty finger while Donnie is running a hand through his unruly hair and waggling his eyebrows as Marlene, the owner of the corner store, walks past him.

Just as I suspected, McKenna's eyes dart between us, putting two and two together.

"I swear they didn't act like that when we were in school," Kristina rushes to explain before turning her glare back on me. "I'm the older sister—"

"By five freaking minutes," I hiss.

"And you've been ratting me out since we were born. Here, McKenna, let me show you a picture from our senior year spring break."

"Kristina." I growl a warning as my sister reaches for her phone.

In my defense, that picture was taken over a decade ago and I was extremely drunk. Who hasn't worn a leotard and tutu while drunk? I mean, so what if I knew every word to *Barbie Girl* by Aqua?

"Twins?" McKenna squeaks, pulling both of our attention back to her.

"You didn't know?"

"I thought you were—Justin is—same last name—"

"You thought—that's gross!" I frown at my sister's overreaction because yeah the idea is gross, but *I'm* not gross. I'm one hell of a catch to anyone who isn't blood related.

"Justin is my nephew," I clarify, rolling my lips to keep from smiling at the shock on her face.

"I thought you knew," Kristina adds.

"I didn't," McKenna says as her eyes find mine. "I thought—"

"That my husband was hitting on you every chance he got." Sympathy fills my sister's eyes. "That's why you made the home visit last week?"

"I was concerned, but then I got there, and everything seemed find. It made me think that you weren't together and just really good at co-parenting, but it's still messy. I didn't want—" She clamps her mouth closed as if she realized she said too much. "I'm going to go back to the animal pen."

"I'll walk you. Justin is trying to get that little girl to do a headstand in her Easter dress," I say, glaring at my sister before giving McKenna my full attention.

"Jesus." Kristina huffs before turning to run after her deviant kid. "Justin Wayne Alexander! Stop right this minute."

I chuckle. "My sister has her hands full with that one."

"He's an incredible little boy, if a little misguided sometimes." Her lips form a weak smile, but her eyes stay pointed to the ground as we walk across the park.

"You really thought I was Justin's dad?"

She shrugs. "I see a lot of the same mannerisms. He's cocky. So are you."

"I guess he kind of sees me as a father figure. His dad took off before he was born."

"So, twins? Any other siblings?"

I don't want to talk about my siblings, but I'll take an in wherever she offers. At least she isn't frowning at me and shooting me down.

"We have an older brother, Miles. He was in the Marine Corps for a while. He's settled in New Mexico. He's a member of a motorcycle club and has a son of his own."

"But you're from here?"

"Born and raised," I answer. "Some people leave and never look back. That's what Miles did. He comes around for holidays occasionally. We talk on the phone every couple of weeks, but he has no interest in living here again. Kristina and I left for college, and for some reason were drawn right back here. I finished graduate school at Lindell University. Small-town life just fits us, you know?"

McKenna hums in agreement.

"What about you? We're literally a tiny dot on the map. How did you find Lindell?"

"I was looking for a job. One opened up here. I came from Dallas."

"Wow. So, this place is a huge culture shock to you, huh?"

"You could say that." The wind rustles her hair once again, but she pushes the strand out of her face before I get the chance to. "At first I hated it. The selection is so thin. One store, one salon, one pizza place, one tiny diner. The coffee place doesn't have a drive-thru. That guy at the gift shop is always trying to sell me a bong when I go in there. It's just different, but then I took the time to actually look around me, and I realized these people are genuine. They don't smile at you when you walk down the street because they feel obligated. They're actually happy to see someone. That little old man at the post office helped me carry my packages inside the other day."

"Watch out for Old Man Hinkle," I warn. "Have you caught him talking to the tree yet?"

"The raccoon?"

"What?"

"The raccoon that lives in the big tree outside the post office?"

"There's a raccoon?"

"He said there was, but I'm a city girl. I know better than to go approach a wild animal. I just nodded my head and smiled when he told me about it."

I dart my eyes in the direction of the post office, but we're too far away for me to verify right now. I'm certain the geezer is full of it, but maybe I am wrong.

"Marlene at the corner store started stocking my favorite candy bar. I mean she keeps them in the back but—"

"What's your favorite candy bar?" I ask, my hackles going up because I went just yesterday to get a—

"Choco snaps," she answers.

"That dirty old bag," I mutter.

"Hmm?"

"Oh nothing." If I have to miss out on my favorite candy because McKenna is eating it all, then it's a sacrifice I'm willing to make. At least until I see Marlene again. That woman has some explaining to do. "Brothers and sisters?"

"I have—"

"Oh, this way," I urge, steering her away from the Tate brothers before they set their eyes on her. If she thinks my flirting is aggressive, she hasn't seen a thing.

"Thanks," she says, thinking I was helping her avoid a swarm of people fighting over who's next in line for a funnel cake. "I have a lot of cousins, but no siblings."

"Will you go out with me?"

"I don't think—" Her mouth closes as she looks around. We're behind the vendors' area. The only people who are going to witness my next rejection are the vendors running back and forth to vehicles to resupply during the lunch rush.

"Then don't think," I say as I step closer.

Her back hits the chicharron food tent, but I'm willing to look past the sound of frying pig fat if she is.

"Just say yes."

"Kalen, I—"

"One date," I beg. "I want to show you that I'm not some bumbling idiot."

"That's not a good idea. You're—"

"The uncle of one of your students?"

"Right," she whispers, like it's going to take a little more time to come to terms with that after thinking since day one that I was his father.

"I'll think about it, but I—"

I press my mouth to hers because I just have to. I can no longer stand here and watch her perfect lips make excuse after excuse after excuse.

There's no tongue—much to my dismay—but there is passion, fire, and so much chemistry it makes a groan rumble from my constricted chest. She clings to me, coming up on the tip of her toes to press harder, a tiny little whimper that does crazy things to my body escaping her lips.

Then she shoves me away, her eyes wide like we just got caught naked in the park by Sheriff Hodson.

I grin at her.

"That was nice."

"That was sneaky," she argues. "I thought the kiss didn't happen until after the date."

"So, there will be a date?"

Her eyes dart all around as if she has to verify for a second time that no one saw us. I could open my mouth and tell her that nothing happens in this town without at least one witness, but she'll find that out soon enough.

"I didn't agree to a date." Her hands begin to straighten her shirt like I mauled her.

I'm going to blow this girl's mind if she thinks for a second that was wild.

"I'll pick you up at seven."

"I didn't agree to a date, Kalen Alexander," she snaps.

But just before she disappears around the tent, her eyes find mine once again. They sparkle with mischief and promises, and I realize that after so much time and so many fails, I've finally got my foot in the door.

Chapter 11
McKenna

I didn't agree to a date. Actually, I flat out refused, so why am I putting my body through the motions of getting ready?

I said no, but I still showered, shaving my entire legs instead of just to the knee. I freaking moisturized for heaven's sake. What is wrong with me?

I distract myself by flitting around the kitchen, wiping counters, and cleaning the front of my appliances, but my brain stays busy. They're siblings, not in a relationship, and with that information, everything I built up against Kalen crumbles. I have no excuse now, and the ones I was holding onto before finding out the truth were on shaky ground already.

I want to date the man. I want to spend more time with him. He's adorable when he trips over his words. He's persistent and charming in a way I never thought I'd find appealing.

"He's also very popular with the ladies," I mutter, recalling watching him at the bar last week surrounded by smiling, expectant women.

And his lips are softer than I could've ever guessed.

I groan my frustrations, blaming the spot at the base of the coffee pot that refuses to be wiped away.

My hair, curled, of course, since I'm staying home this evening—even I roll my eyes at this lie—bounces against my shoulders as I scrub harder.

He may be very good looking and charming and his eyes may be the perfect shade of blue. He may have hair that I've been tempted to run my fingers through more than once, locks so luscious Dr. McDreamy would be envious. He may have a smile—one that's a little crocked and endearing—that has invaded my dreams more than once, but none of that matters.

Lindell is a small town, and even if I forget about the townsfolk's penchant for gossip, if things go south, it will makes things weird for me. He's still going to be involved in Justin's life, even though he isn't his father. I'm still going to see him nearly every day until summer break, and even then he's going to be around town.

And that's the real issue. I'm worried about seeing him everywhere and not being with him.

I keep scrubbing, so certain that keeping my hands busy will eventually keep my mind from working overtime.

It doesn't.

But then the phone rings, and it's just what I need to distract myself from thoughts of Kalen "stupid smile" Alexander.

"Hello?" I say into the phone the second it's pressed to my ear.

I didn't recognize the number, but I'll talk to a telemarketer about my vehicle warranty for an hour at this point. Anything is better than thoughts of *him*.

"McKenna?" I tilt my head. Her voice is familiar, but I can't place it.

"This is she."

"Hi, this is Rebecca Shears. We met at the Brew and Chew on Monday."

"Yes, ma'am. How are you?" I don't know if this is the distraction I need because this woman wants me to date her son, but I'll take what I can get.

"Just fine, dear, but I have a problem."

I remain silent. Does she really think I'm going to volunteer to help when I have no clue what's going on?

She waits me out, and that bamboozled feeling I got with her at the diner returns.

"How can I help?" I ask eventually.

This woman is good.

"I'm hoping you can help me with some gift baskets for the Jubilee."

"The what?"

"The Lindell Jubilee, dear. My dining room looks like a gift store. There's no way I can get all of this done in time. Are you free this evening?"

"Yes!" I yell in a rush.

She laughs on the other end of the line. "I love your enthusiasm, dear. What a blessing you are to our community."

What she doesn't know is she just gave me an out for the date I wasn't going on with Kalen. He'll knock, and I won't answer because I'll be gone.

She gives me her address, and I realize, just like everything else around here, it's within walking distance from my house. I assure her I'll be there in fifteen minutes.

I change out of the dress I have no business wearing for a night planned watching television, and head in that direction.

"Mrs. Shears," I greet when she steps out onto the front porch before I can make my way up the sidewalk. She must've been waiting for me, and that should be a red flag because for a woman so busy she's drowning in gift baskets, she should be inside working.

"Rebecca, please." She clasps my hands the same way she did in the diner, only this time I have to wonder if she's doing it to keep me from running.

I look past her toward the door, but don't see anyone else. "Is this a setup?"

"A what, dear?"

I bite the inside of my cheek to keep from smiling. She's not fooling anyone with her wide eyes and faux confused look.

"Is your son inside?" I won't walk away, but I need to know if

I'm going to be ambushed.

"Of course not, dear. My husband is here. Does that make you uncomfortable? Have you heard rumors?" She shifts to the side, my hands still clasped in hers as she guides me up the porch and into the house. "I love my town dearly, but so many of the folks around here have loose lips. They'll gossip about anything, and if there isn't something juicy to spread around, they'll make something up. He's really not that bad. You'll see."

I'm thinking I'm walking into some sort of trap, something worse, more sinister than a man wanting a date. If I think reasonably, I imagine her son would be annoyed with his mother trying to set him up with a woman.

A grin spreads across my face when I step inside. The house is big and airy. Lived in but tidy. The scent of spring flowers hangs heavy in the air but light enough that it isn't overpowering.

"George!" Mrs. Shears bellows. "Come meet McKenna!"

There's a crash at the back of the house, but Mrs. Shears chuckles instead of rushing to see if the man is alright.

More sounds of things knocking together come from a room down the hall before a man appears. He has goggles on, making his eyes look like those of a bug.

"He fancies himself a scientist, dear." Mrs. Shears pats my hand as if she's afraid I'll bolt.

The slight man approaches, head tilted back as if looking through the bottom part of the goggle lenses will help him see me better.

"George, this is McKenna Kaiser, the new teacher down at the school."

"Lovely to meet you," I say, holding out my hand when Mrs. Shears finally releases it.

"She's not here for the new lip enhancers."

Mrs. Shears sighs. "No, George. She's here to help with the gift baskets."

George nods, patting my hand much the same his wife did before turning back around and disappearing back into the room down the hall.

"He rarely comes out of his *laboratory*," Mrs. Shears explains, saying the last word like it's a running joke in the family. "Everything is just in here."

She wasn't joking when she said things were out of control. Her dining room table is lost under the different items, piles of baskets, tissue paper, and spools of ribbon.

"Is there a process? A certain method to loading the gift baskets?" I ask, ready to dive in.

"We have to split the items up, so we won't have an all animal basket or a snack basket. A little variety in each is the best way to go."

I take a step closer and pick up one of the wicker baskets. "I feel like there's a story there."

She grins. "Many people in town donate, and for some weird reason want their donations back, so they bid on those baskets only. We discovered what they were doing a couple years back and after we split the baskets up, people were more likely to bid on multiple ones. It really drives the price up. We've nearly doubled our fundraising each year since."

"They don't stop donating?" That's what people would do where I was raised.

"Not a chance. They'd rather be known for overspending on a basket than being called cheap by the others in town. If you haven't learned it yet, you'll soon come to realize everything in Lindell is a competition. Even you, my dear."

"Me?"

"Yes. I heard about your conversation with the Tate brothers." Oh, Lord. "And your interaction with Theodore."

I tilt my head in confusion. "Theodore?"

"Theodore Hinkle? You chatted with him outside the post office two weeks ago."

I huff a laugh. "Mr. Hinkle is trying to date me?"

She smiles wide as she reaches for a spool of gold ribbon. "Of course. He's single after all."

"I'm flattered," I say, recalling the way Mr. Hinkle patted my shoulder as we parted ways.

"You need to look out for those Tate brothers. They're... odd."

I keep quiet as I gather a handful of different items and begin to situate them in the basket.

Mrs. Shears can't stand the silence. "They date the same woman. It was cute when they were younger, but they're over thirty now. Their momma is fit to be tied. We all know they're never going to find a woman willing to date two men at the same time."

So it is true!

"Everyone in town knows about their... preferences?"

"Yes, dear."

For someone who was unhappy earlier about gossip where George was concerned, Mrs. Shears has no problem doing her fair share of it herself. I learn about Stanley Jones—AKA Hippie Jones—and how he was straitlaced and ready to face the world when he left for college but came back with long hair and different ideals about life. Apparently, the commune he was a part of in Vermont where he went to college is to blame. But she tells the story with a smile on her face and not a hint of disapproval in her voice.

"And don't get me started on Harvey and Ethel Dunbar."

I keep my eyes on my work, tying the ribbon on the basket the way she showed me earlier.

I want the story. I need the story and I don't even know the Dunbars. I know she'll cave, eventually.

Mrs. Shears comes around to my side of the table.

"You've seen Abe Fisher's teeth, right?"

Oh! This is the gossip I needed.

"I have." I nod, giving nothing away even though I'm dancing inside my skin.

I don't know when I became the woman who wants the scoop on the people in town, but my heart rate kicks up in anticipation.

"Well, Ethel was—"

The front door swings open, causing Mrs. Shears to snap her jaw closed, and I want to growl at the person interrupting. When my eyes fall on a smiling Kalen Alexander, I actually do growl.

"Good of you to stop by," Mrs. Shears says with a grumble.

Maybe he's here to pick up some baskets because the alternative wouldn't suit me well. I like spending time here, and there's enough work to be done that one day won't be enough. I'd hate to have to decline if invited again because Mrs. Shears is his—

"Good sons don't stay away for so long."

"Mom, I was here two days ago."

Crash and burn.

Damn it!

I keep my eyes on the basket, fluffing the bow I tied even though I need to set it aside and get started on another one. That would require getting closer to him since the empty baskets are on the end of the table near where he's standing.

"Why is she—did you not apologize, Kalen? I taught you better than that."

Oh, God. They've talked about me?

"I apologized. Didn't I, McKenna?"

"For umm?" Kissing me earlier? My cheeks heat with having those thoughts in front of his mother because the kiss affected me more than it should have.

"For spilling beer on your boots."

"You really shouldn't be drinking so much," Mrs. Shears chastises. "My son can be a fool sometimes."

"It's fine." I look at Mrs. Shears in an attempt to avoid making eye contact with Kalen. "He's the one you wanted me to go out with?"

"Despite his recent actions, he really is a great guy." She pats his cheek a little too hard, and he winces at the warning but stands there and takes it with a grin on his face. When he winks at me, I have to look away. "I didn't mention his name because I wanted you to know we were a normal family."

"Has she met George?" Kalen asks with a quick laugh.

Mrs. Shears glares at him before turning away. "I have to go grab some more ribbon."

I stare at the piles of ribbon at the end of the table as she makes a hasty exit. The woman isn't as sly as she thinks she is.

I manage to ignore him as he moves closer, hating that I changed out of the nice dress. I'm in a t-shirt and leggings, struggling not to straighten my clothes.

"McKenna?" His voice is a purr that I feel in my bones.

"Hmm?"

"Look at me." He doesn't even give me time to angle my head before his strong hand cups my jaw.

His lips are on mine once again. The kiss is soft and sweet, a promise of sorts that leaves me wanting more when he pulls away.

"We're supposed to be on a date."

"I'm helping your mother."

"The Jubilee isn't for two months. She's got this under control."

I can't even be mad at the woman for being sneaky and getting me over here, not with him standing so close I can smell his spicy cologne. It's as intoxicating as his smile.

"I didn't agree to a date."

"But you want to go." His fingers twist in the hair hanging over my shoulder. "Damn, you're gorgeous."

It doesn't feel like a line, one he'd say to get my attention. It feels like a declaration, something he just has to say.

"Okay," I whisper.

"Okay?" He's giddy, and it makes me smile.

"Sure." I shrug, an attempt at indifference that isn't fooling either of us.

Next thing I know, his hand is in mine and he's tugging me

toward the front door. I don't even have time to argue about telling his mother goodbye, and when I look back at the house, Mrs. Shears is standing in the doorway with a triumphant grin on her face.

"Did you plan this?"

"The date? Of course, I did."

"No, the ambush at your parents' house."

He stops on the sidewalk near his truck, both of his hands cupping my face. I do my best not to lean into the touch. "I didn't know you were here, but I won't lie and say I'm disappointed." His lips brush mine once again, but my brain is too fried right now to consider his mother who is still no doubt watching from the doorway.

"You can't keep kissing me like that," I say, a little breathless and not wanting his affection to end at all.

He doesn't listen as he lowers his mouth once again. I turn my head, cheeks flaming with unnamed emotions. He nuzzles my neck with his nose, and I have no damn business getting turned on by this man in broad daylight in front of his mother. I clear my throat, and he takes the hint, tugging open the passenger door of his truck with a gesture for me to climb inside.

The drive is quiet, Kalen's hand finding mine across the bench seat, and I let it happen, tangling our fingers together like this is date one hundred instead of the first. Why am I so comfortable around him? What happened to all the arguments I formed about dating him?

"The park?" I ask when he pulls into the nearly empty parking lot.

The area has been cleaned from the day's festivities.

"Were you expecting something different?"

"No," I answer honestly because the park is perfect and public. God knows I need to be out in the open with him and not tucked away any place private.

He climbs out, coming around to my side. After I jump down, he opens the back door to the quad-cab truck and pulls out an old-fashioned basket. I may not have been planning to be home for the date he insisted on, but it seems this man is prepared.

I can't help the laugh that bubbles from my throat. "A picnic?"

He winks again, and it isn't as cheesy as the last time he did it.

He leads us to a tree on the far side of the park, managing to keep our fingers tangled as we walk, only releasing me once we get to our destination so he can spread out a small blanket he had tucked away in the top of the basket.

If I saw this in a romantic movie, I'd scoff at the idea. A picnic in a park? This has to be the corniest idea ever, but somehow in the moment, it's adorably perfect.

He busies himself pulling plastic bowls of various foods from the basket before sitting down and offering me his hand once again. I join him on the blanket, bottom lip tucked between my teeth to keep from smiling.

"My mother likes you."

"I just wanted to help, but now it feels like a test."

"You didn't know she was my mother?" He laughs when I shake my head. "She's normally trying to convince women to date me."

"Oh, she did that, but she never told me your name."

Kalen presses a cold grape to my mouth, and when I open my mouth to eat it, his fingers brush my lips. It feels much more sexual than it has any right to feel, and when his eyes lock with mine as I chew, butterflies swarm in my belly.

"My dad died when I was little." Well, that information is sobering. "She remarried George when Kristina and I were in junior high. The man is a nut job, but I love him."

"He's a scientist?"

Kalen chuckles, and the sound rumbling from his chest brings a smile to my face.

"Scientist? No, but he does tinker with everything. My mom has to change the passwords to the computers on a regular basis to keep track of his spending. The man will buy just about any concoction found online, so sure he can add a little of this and a little of that to make something better. He nearly burns down the house weekly."

Conversation between us is easy as we laugh and eat the fruit, cheese, and deli meat he packed in the basket. He's an open book, answering every question I have and never deflecting when I think he might. I don't know that I've ever met a man so open.

As the sun fades, we laugh and joke, telling stories from our childhoods until I get a shiver from the cool spring air.

"I should take you home."

I want to argue, but home sounds good... and private. I don't think that the privacy I was avoiding earlier is such a bad idea right now.

Instead of climbing back into his truck, we walk. The tangle of our fingers feels more intimate than it ever has, and by the time we make it to my front door, my body is on fire, anticipation swimming through my veins like liquid lava. A couple hours of laughing and my body is on fire for this man. I don't question the need heating me up. It just feels right, meant to be in a way I don't understand.

When he leans in to press his mouth to mine, I quickly wrap my arms around his neck and pull him closer. The picnic basket in his grip clatters to my front steps, but we both ignore it.

When his tongue sweeps across mine for the very first time, it's as if I've been struck by lightning. We groan in unison, his arms wrapping around my back. He's enjoying the kiss as much as I am if I go by how his body is reacting to mine. It's a heady feeling to be desired by this man.

His teeth nip at my lower lip before he dives back in, and the butterflies that were fluttering in my stomach earlier turn into a swarm of need.

"Kalen," I pant against his mouth.

I feel his smile against my lips, but then he pulls away, only as far as my grip around his neck will allow. When he presses his forehead to mine, his breath rushing past his lips, I know what he's going to say. I open my mouth to argue. Going inside together is the best idea in the world. I feel his body's reaction to me. I know he wants it just as much.

"We'll get to the good stuff, beautiful, but I want to do this right."

Although I'm needy and feeling borderline desperate, I nod, releasing him when he takes a step back.

"Your mouth." His thumb sweeps over my lower lip. "I don't think I'll ever get enough."

I swallow thickly, shoving down a tease about what my mouth is capable of, and then he's kissing me again.

His hands run lower on my back, hands getting dangerously close to gripping my butt. I swallow his groan when I press into him, his thickness stiff against my lower belly.

"McKenna." His hands are on my shoulders, using them to urge me back a step, but I don't feel insulted. His kiss-swollen lips turn up into a smile, his breathing heavy. "Can I have your phone number?"

"You can have anyth—"

"Just your number for tonight," he says, the look in his eyes telling me he's a little remorseful for saying the words.

We trade phones, and I grin down at his after he hands it over without pause. Most of the men I dated in the past guard theirs, not wanting their secrets to be disclosed.

I type my name and number into his contact list, and he does the same on mine before we exchange them again.

When he leans in for a kiss, he presses one to my cheek, and I envy his restraint, as I have none left to offer.

I grin down at him as he reaches for the picnic basket.

"You better not send me pictures of your junk," I warn, but honestly, I don't think I'd be offended.

"I won't, but feel free to send me pictures of your everything."

He winks again before walking away.

I watch him as he disappears down the street, hearing his happy whistle long after he's gone.

Chapter 12

Kalen

"Score!" Collins says as soon as I step into my classroom. His hands shoot up, making the universal sign for a touchdown.

His best friend and Lindell University track star Huxley Shaw grumbles about being down several points, but even their juvenile antics won't dampen my mood this morning.

Mondays usually suck. Mondays after town events are normally even worse, but my night ended with my lips on McKenna, tongue tangled with hers. The threat of an apocalypse couldn't make the smile slide from my face. I'd face zombies with enthusiasm at this point.

I check the time on my cell phone, hating that there are still fifteen minutes before class begins. That's the only issue I've had since leaving McKenna standing on her front porch. Time has slowed to a crawl. I have an entire day before I get to see her when I pick Justin up from school, and I already know the day is going to drag.

God, that woman. The look in her eyes last night. The way she pressed her hips to mine.

She's mesmerizing. A gift sent from heaven forcing me to do things in my shower I haven't done in years. I smile wider as I picture her flushed cheeks from last night. Best freaking Easter, hands down.

"You're such a jerk," Collins snaps when I begin to walk past him.

"A jerk?" My grin doesn't fade. "How so?"

"You banged the teacher."

That'll do it. "How do you figure?"

Huxley turns his attention to two girls in the desks in front of him, and I begin to wonder how much trouble I'd get into for putting my cousin in a headlock and insisting he never bring McKenna up in conversation again.

He points to my face. "No man is that happy on a Monday morning for any other reason than getting laid the night before."

My eyes narrow, but so does his.

"Or this morning. Did you spend the entire night wrapped up in Ms. Kaiser?"

"You need to keep your voice down," I hiss, taking a menacing step closer. Of course, it doesn't faze my cousin. "I didn't spend the night with McKenna, but if I did, it wouldn't be any business of yours."

"So, you just walked her home after your little park picnic and kissed her on her front porch steps?"

His question has way too many details, but I shouldn't be surprised. This is Lindell after all.

"I was a total gentleman." My thoughts weren't gentlemanly, but my actions were.

"A wuss, you mean."

"And you're going to tell me that if Oakleigh Guthrie ever gave you the time of day you'd ruin it by jumping in bed with her the first chance you got?"

His smile widens, and it's the opposite reaction I expect.

"Are you that bad at sex?"

"You little shit," I hiss.

He jerks back, hand going to his chest, an action I've seen my mother do too many times to still have any effect on me. "Mr. Alexander!"

I cross my arms over my chest. Collins is always so dramatic the girls in the room don't pull their eyes from Huxley to pay him any attention. They're used to his antics. It's when his voice lowers, a clear indication that he doesn't want to be heard, that ears begin to perk up.

"Are you so bad at sex that things would be ruined once you do the deed?" A devious grin spreads across his face. "I can give you some pointers."

I walk away. I'm confident in my bedroom skills, and this guy isn't in a place to understand what I mean about being casual with a woman I don't want to be casual with.

Thank God Oakleigh is ignoring him. He'd ruin things with her the first chance he gets if she paid him any attention. Sex is great and all but jumping right into it when it isn't the end goal is foolish.

More students begin to trickle in as Huxley and Collins go back to thumping a paper football between goalposts they're making with their hands.

Huxley thumps one a little too hard, and it goes over Collins' head.

My hands still over my pile of papers as I watch it hit Oakleigh in the chin before sliding down the front of her shirt. She glares, not at Huxley, but at Collins as if it was his plan all along.

Collins snaps to his feet once he realizes what happened.

"Shit! Let me help you."

His hand is slapped away before he can reach for the paper football. "Touch me and die."

Collins' head snaps back, only unlike he did with me earlier, his reaction isn't rehearsed. He's genuinely shocked at her growl. Was he really going to reach down her shirt for the stupid thing? I make a mental note to talk to him about boundaries. The guy is a sexual harassment lawsuit waiting to happen.

Without pulling the thing from her blouse, Oakleigh walks straight past him toward her normal seat in the front row.

"Good morning, Professor," she says as she walks past me.

"Good morning, Oakleigh. I hope you had a good weekend."

She nods but doesn't say anything further before settling in her seat.

"Did you see that?"

I whip my head around finding Collins standing a little too close for comfort.

"She was seconds away from clawing your eyes."

"Thin line between love and hate," he says, his grin never falling from his face.

"And the Great Wall of China only averages fifteen feet wide and yet it can still be seen from space."

His nose scrunches up. "You watch too much Jeopardy. Did you see her notebook?"

I sigh. "I wasn't looking at her notebook."

Anger fills his eyes as he steps in front of me, blocking my view of his infatuation. "Then what the hell were you looking at, Kalen?"

"Her eyes, you idiot, like normal people do when they speak to others. They're those two things about a foot above the other two things you always seem to notice first."

"I'm a breast man," he offers with a shrug, making me realize the guy is hopeless.

"I need to start class, Collins. Go find a seat."

"Her notebook! It has a Lenny sticker on it."

"So does nearly every notebook carried by every student." I shake my hands like I'm a cheerleader holding pom-poms. "School spirit and all that."

"She likes me, man."

"She likes Lenny."

He leans closer. "I am Lenny."

"Lenny is an idea," I argue. "That's why the school doesn't want to put a name and face to the person in the costume. Lenny is a tradition, not just one guy."

"If she knew—"

The look in my eyes makes him snap his jaw shut. I still don't know who wore that damned costume the years I attended here, and I'll be damned if he's going to let some girl he's crushing on find out if I didn't.

"Find your seat, Collins. Maybe if you want the girl to notice you, stop acting like this is your seventh year in high school. You're a month away from being a college senior."

He glares at me. "I'm telling Aunt Becca you're in love with McKenna."

He rushes away before I can threaten him because I know he'll do it just to make my life more difficult.

My mother hearing such news doesn't carry the same regret as it did with Beth. That woman is nuts. I don't want McKenna to hear such things because I don't want her to be scared away.

Collins effectively avoids eye contact with me through the entire class, and he sneaks out before I can grab him and threaten him with bodily harm.

Mom knows I like McKenna, and if she didn't before yesterday, then the kiss in front of her house explained it all. But my mom thinking it's more than just dating would mean plans put into action. McKenna may have been ready to invite me into her bed last night, but she's a great distance away from being okay with *Save the Date* cards and wedding dress shopping.

Chapter 13

McKenna

I'm putting off the inevitable but laugh again at the images Kalen has been sending me all week.

He's texted, asking me to meet him in town for dinner every night, but I decline. My cheeks heat from embarrassment every time I think about how I acted like a sex-deprived saucy minx Sunday night on my front porch steps. I was ready to jump his bones at the slightest hint that he was willing. That's going to take some time to get over.

Going by the images he keeps sending, I don't think he's the slightest bit deterred by the distance I've tried to put between us. The thread is a continuous line of pictures. They're not peen pics, but they might as well be. I've been sent eggplant images and images that at first glance look sexual but upon closer inspection aren't. The one I keep going back to, however, is a video. It starts out with the camera moving in slow motion over tan thickness. The first time I watched it the vein made my mouth water. Then the camera zooms out to disclose it's a dang hot pretzel. I laughed, then watched it ten more times. It still manages to turn me on as I watch it again.

I'm killing time before going back to help Mrs. Shears with more gift baskets. Thankfully, she didn't ask me about leaving with Kalen on Sunday when she called, but I doubt I'll be able to avoid the inquisition once she has me in front of her. I almost text Kalen to ask what she may know, but I don't want to tell him I'm going back over there.

I'm legitimately going to help her, but at the same time, it feels like I'm invading his space, putting myself right in the middle of his family. It feels a little creepy and invasive, but I know I'm going to go because I promised I would. Hopefully, he'll either stay away or if he doesn't, I pray he doesn't see it as a forced infiltration.

I head out a little early, keeping my legs to a leisurely stroll as I walk to the Shears' house. His truck isn't outside, and I shove down the hint of disappointment it makes me feel.

Mrs. Shears once again meets me on the porch. This time when her hands clasp mine in greeting there's a softness in her eyes, as if she knows secrets I'm not privileged to.

We get to work on baskets right away, because in the days since I was last here, the things on her table have more than doubled. At this rate, there will be enough baskets for every woman, man, and child in the entire town.

"How popular is this event?" I ask, as I tie a ribbon on the tenth basket I've made since arriving.

"Huge." She beams like the success of the entire event is all her doing. "It's the biggest fundraiser of the year, and that's saying a lot because there's always some type of event going on."

"The Easter egg hunt was a fundraiser, too, wasn't it?"

She nods. "Nearly everything going on in Lindell is an effort to raise money. The Jubilee, the scavenger hunt, and donkey basketball are the most entertaining. There's something for everyone to do, and I—"

"Donkey basketball?" I chuckle. "It is what it sounds like?"

"Exactly, but that doesn't happen until late July. We can't use the gymnasium until right before the yearly upkeep on the floors going into the new school year. You'll love it. The whole town comes out to watch."

I nod in agreement, but sadness hits my chest. There are only six weeks of school left, and although all the other teachers have gotten contracts for the next year, my box in the teacher workroom has remained empty. I knew coming here for only a couple of months was a gamble, but I was desperate to start my career. When I signed the contract that carried me through the end of this school year, I knew there was a chance Mrs. Eaton would come back to her classroom. What I didn't expect was Kalen Alexander and how easy it was for him to crawl under my skin. There's a very good chance I won't even be here to experience dating him or the thrill of donkey basketball.

Sadness washes over me as we continue to pack gift baskets.

"After we finish all the baskets, we'll get started on the mesh wreaths," Mrs. Shears says as she stacks another basket near the front door.

"Where are you storing all these?"

"Kalen takes them to the community center for me." She smiles but doesn't bring up her son again.

Somehow, the meddling mother must feel like she's done her part and isn't anxious to try and get me to go out on a date with him any longer.

"Doesn't he make the most gorgeous glassware?" she asks when I look down at the bong in my hand.

Surely she knows what they're for, but just in case she doesn't, I keep my lips zipped closed.

"It is beautiful." I'm adding the blue and green bong to the basket I'm making when the front door swings open.

Excitement fills my body as I wait to see who is walking inside, and a wide grin spans my entire face when Kalen walks in.

"Good to see you, dear. We've been working hard. You'll probably have to make two trips this time." Kalen keeps his eyes on mine as his mother presses a quick kiss to his cheek.

"McKenna, you remember my son, Kalen."

I roll my lips between my teeth.

"Of course, she does, Mom. How could she forget her boyfriend?"

He closes the distance, pressing his mouth to mine before I can argue.

There's no tongue like our last kiss, but it still feels more intimate than acceptable in front of his mother.

"Boyfriend?" I whisper against his lips.

He answers me with another peck before stepping to my side and wrapping his arms around my waist.

Mrs. Shears is standing across the room with her hands clasped under her chin like the sight of us standing together is just too precious for her to handle.

"I knew it! You two are perfect for each other."

"And it looks like you've been working so hard, you're running low on ribbon."

I glance to the pile at the end of the table when Mrs. Shears speaks up. "I've got more in the craft room!"

And she's gone, just like last time.

"I've missed you," Kalen whispers as he repositions himself in front of my body.

His lips are on me once again. This time, he doesn't waste a second sliding his slick tongue past my lips, and I groan at his eagerness. My hands find the nape of his neck as his skate down my back, fingers digging into my clothes.

He pulls away before I'm done, and my mouth is still hanging open when his mother rejoins us. He presses a final kiss just below my ear in that perfect spot that makes my knees weak before backing away.

We work through a dozen more baskets as he loads his truck, making, as promised, two trips to and from the community center.

He sighs but there's no frustration in the effort when he comes back the second time to see another round of baskets needing to be loaded up.

I hate that all the baskets are done, and the dining room is cleared, but then I remember Mrs. Shears mentioning making wreaths, so I imagine it won't be long before I'm invited over once again to help with those.

As Kalen places the last of the baskets in his truck, Mrs. Shear shuffles me toward the living room with the promise of sweet tea and fresh-baked cookies.

"I like seeing you in my childhood home," Kalen whispers as he settles next to me on the sofa.

I grin, resisting the urge to tell him that I love being here. I already feel time ticking away, each second bringing us closer to goodbye—not just tonight but when my contract ends with the school.

Mrs. Shears joins us, a tray of iced teas and cookies in her hands, and she begins to tell Kalen about all the work we've been putting into the baskets. He listens intently, not once showing a hint of disinterest in his mother describing each item we've encountered. He even laughs when she mentions the two dozen "vases" Hippie Jones donated.

He respects her, and I've always wanted a man like that, having encountered too many men who are quick to roll their eyes at just the mention of their parents.

George never pokes his head out of his laboratory, but we can hear muttered curses and an occasional crash. Neither Kalen nor Mrs. Shears seem concerned enough to check on him, so I don't worry either.

After an hour, I excuse myself to the restroom, needing a moment to myself more than anything. It would be too easy to fall in love with that man, his family, and this town, and I can't seem to stop myself. Who knew that a little slice of perfection was only an hour away from Austin, Texas, tucked away in the middle of nowhere, beside a crook in the Colorado River?

"Hey."

I gasp, startled to find Kalen waiting for me in the hallway. He smiles as he inches forward, pressing my back against the wall.

"You okay?"

I'm too distracted by his mouth as it trails down my neck to be concerned with having to walk away from him all too soon.

"I'm good." He nips at my shoulder. "So very good."

His chuckle is light, his warm breath floating over my skin settling the desperation in my bones. This man, damn it, he knows exactly what I need.

"Do you still have a room here?"

He groans at the suggestion, his hips rolling against me.

"I'd love to see it."

He looks pained when he pulls his head back.

"That can't happen, city girl."

He kisses me again, and it feels like an apology, as if he's tortured knowing there's a room up there that we can't sneak away to.

"No?" I prod.

"We don't do things like that in Lindell. What would the neighbors say?"

His lips continue their assault on my neck.

"You're saying you've never had a girl in your room before?"

He shakes his head. "The rule is no one without a ring on their left hand can go up the stairs."

My heart pounds in my chest, so loud I'm certain he can hear the unsteady beat. Why does the idea of him proposing thrill me?

"So all the single women in town are virgins waiting on a proposal?" I tease, feeling his mouth turn up into a smile against my cheek. "The poor women considering a date with the Tate brothers. Such a shame."

I press myself closer, flattening my breasts against him, all the while wondering if he can feel the hardened tips through my shirt.

He groans again, agonized over needing to end this sooner than he wants.

"Kalen?"

The man is slow to step away from me even at the sound of his mother's voice.

"Did you say something about marriage?"

Chapter 14

Kalen

I swear my mother is like a dog with a damned bone.

"Come on," I say, taking a regretful step back from McKenna and clasping her hand in mine. "I hope you don't scare easily."

She laughs and I love the sound echoing down the narrow hallway.

I could've predicted what I was going to find in the living room, but when I see my mother sitting with a photo album in her lap and five more stacked on the table in front of her, I don't cringe. It's a first for me.

"What do you have?" McKenna asks as she takes a seat close to my mother.

The two of them on the sofa, taking space in the middle doesn't leave any room for me, and I'm more than a little salty about it. McKenna smiles in my direction when I huff and plop down in George's mostly unused recliner.

"I wanted to show you some pictures," Mom says, opening the hard cover on the photo album in her lap. "Kalen has always been a good-looking kid."

I huff, knowing she's full of it, and wondering if my girl will run out the front door when she gets to the third book. Junior high is awkward for everyone, right? I haven't met a single person that was always a gorgeous swan. Although, I doubt McKenna ever had an awkward stage in her life. She's too graceful and pretty to have suffered with acne and teeth that required two sets of braces to fix.

"Do you have to do this?" I grumble. "You're going to scare her off."

"We wouldn't be going through photo albums if you would've taken her up on the suggestion to go upstairs."

My mouth hangs opens, and McKenna's cheeks flush in embarrassment.

How could I forget how thin the dang walls are in this house?

I clear my throat, suddenly becoming very interested in the curtains on the front window.

"That was disrespectful," McKenna says after a long pause. "I shouldn't—"

"It's fine, dear," Mom says, patting her on her leg before spreading the photo album between both their laps. "I remember what it was like. Young love is overpowering, and hormones are sometimes hard to handle. When I was younger—"

"Mom, no!" I snap, but then chuckle. "Can you skip the puberty talk? We're both grown."

Mom tsks at me, but then refocuses. "See? He's always been happy."

The page turns, and instead of wondering what McKenna is seeing for the first time, I keep my attention on her, on the smiles, on the way her eyes crinkle when Mom gives more details than necessary about the time I got curious and stuck my finger in a goat's ass at a petting zoo when I was three. She has tears rolling down her cheeks when Mom mimics the sound that poor goat made. It's insanely accurate, and it still makes me cringe. I've never touched another goat since, having been traumatized by its reaction at such a young age.

By the time Mom makes it to the second book, antics and stories tagging along with each and every picture, McKenna is holding her stomach and gasping for breath.

Clearly, Mom has a way with words and can weave a tale enthralling enough to keep her on the edge of her seat waiting for the punchline. I wish half of what she was saying were fibs, but I was a mischievous kid, and nearly all of it is true.

I don't miss that she skips over the year my father died. No one in the house had much to smile about then, but Mom is a trouper, and was hell-bent to make her children's lives as normal as possible after the loss of a parent. I'm grateful every day that she found George, regardless of the smells currently coming out of his area in the back of the house.

"This was his eighth-grade graduation. Look how handsome he is in a jacket and tie."

McKenna's eyes find mine as she agrees with my mother. "So handsome."

I shift in my seat, the look in her eyes admiring the man I am now. I have no idea how I'm going to keep from following her inside her house later if she extends the offer. If my mom left the room for even a second, I'd drag her up the stairs and fulfill some of the fantasies that have been floating through my mind in recent weeks. Mom all but gave me permission, and I'm ready to run with it.

When Mom looks at the clock, she looks regretful. "I have to get started on dinner. McKenna, you'll join us?"

"I'd love to," she says as Mom takes the fourth photo album from her lap.

"Think you kids can behave long enough for me to get the casserole in the oven?"

"No promises," I tease as I watch McKenna's eyes widen once again.

Mom walks past, patting my cheek as if she thinks I'm joking, and I'll stay in the recliner. If I get up and go to McKenna, she's going to end up over my shoulder and carried away.

"You were a cute kid," she says, her hands primly folded in her lap.

"Even with the braces and wild hair?"

"Even then."

"Mom says I'm going to have adorable babies."

"I bet you will."

I swallow when she doesn't seem afraid of baby talk. I mean, it's no confession that she wants to get started right away, but she doesn't go into a long spiel about wanting to wait until thirty or anything. I'm counting it as a win.

"George always eats dinner with her," I say, changing the

subject because imagining making babies with her is causing problems in my jeans.

"Yeah?" She bites her lower lip. "That's nice."

My nose twitches as I try not to smile. We're both avoiding certain topics, and I like that she's willing to do this with me.

"He was a science professor at Lindell until he retired two years ago."

"He seems like a lovely man."

"Most people find him strange."

"I'd call him dedicated to his passion."

"I'm passionate."

"I bet you are."

"About math."

She raises her eyebrows.

"And teaching."

A smile spreads across her pretty face.

"You could say I'm an expert," I declare, knowing we are no longer talking about work.

"Lots of practice then?"

"Not too much. Just enough to get it right... every time."

"That so?"

I nod.

"What about you?"

"Me?" She points to herself.

"Have a lot of practice?"

"I've practiced some, but never with an expert passionate about their work."

"That so?"

"Unfortunately."

"That's a shame."

"It is. Want to help me practice sometime?"

"Every second of the day."

She shifts in her seat at my answer.

"That's a lot of practice."

"It is." God, I'm hard as a damn rock.

"Think you can turn me into an expert?"

"I get the feeling you're perfect already."

"So, I don't need practice?"

"Probably not."

"That's a shame." She swallows.

"No practice. Maybe a test would be best."

"A comprehensive one?"

"Of course, that's the only way to know your full range of skills."

"Will this be oral or written?"

I nearly groan, and I'd worry if she didn't seem as affected as I am right now, but she's wiggling like she has ants in her pants. "Both."

Her eyelids lower before she speaks again. "So, you'd want me to use my mouth and my hands?"

"Jesus." I scrape a hand over the top of my head before looking in the direction of the kitchen.

"And what about you?"

"Me?"

"Will I get the chance to test you as well?"

"I'll pass with flying colors, both orally and with my hands." Has George set the house on fire because the room is heating up? "I have a special pen I use for such tests."

"Yeah?" I nod. "I'd like to see this pen sometime. Is it reliable?"

"Magical. You'll love it."

"So sure of yourself."

"I'm an expert, remember?"

"So, you keep saying."

"I'm ready when you are, baby."

Her eyes dart to my lap, and I barely resist the urge to spread my legs and give her a hint at what I'm working with.

"McKenna, can you join me in the kitchen?" Mom's voice from the other room makes her eyes snap up.

"Yes, ma'am!" she squeaks, giving me a look as she stands on shaky legs that places the blame of the entire conversation on my shoulders.

"Kalen, don't come in this kitchen until you have control of your erection."

McKenna gasps, her steps faltering.

I laugh, grabbing her hand as she tries to slide past me.

"You're trouble, you know that?"

The second she winks at me is when I fall head over heels in love with this girl.

Chapter 15
McKenna

"And we both have work in the morning," Kalen argues when his mother urges us to stay a little longer.

I'm not over the embarrassment of his mother hearing the innuendo-laced conversation we got wrapped up in when she went to go make dinner.

Dinner was wonderful, something she called a tater tot casserole that had so much cheese in it, my mouth started watering the second she dipped the serving spoon into it. Conversation was wonderful. Mrs. Shears didn't bring up anything too awkward. At least not for me, but her stories about Kalen continued throughout the entire meal. He'd occasionally scoff and correct her when she got a little too exuberant in her tales, but he laughed right along with me, his hand finding my thigh under the table more times than I could count.

George was as normal as I imagine George could be, but it was nice to see him without his prescription goggles, and he looked decidedly less like a bug without them.

I learned so many things today, and as I smiled and laughed, I hated being given so much information. It was only going to make it harder on me when I had to leave.

"It's just one more photo album," Mrs. Shears bargains. "An hour tops."

"An hour I could spend making out with my girlfriend without a meddling mother around the corner."

My cheeks flame again, and I have to turn toward the front door.

"I'll see you on Tuesday, McKenna." I nod in agreement without looking at her. I don't know what I'm going to be doing here Tuesday, but I can't look her in the eye long enough to ask questions.

First the kiss when Kalen first walked in then the offer to go upstairs, all wrapped up with the conversation while she was in the kitchen. This woman must think I'm a wanton, sex-crazed maniac, and maybe I am.

"Goodnight, Mother." Kalen presses his hand to my back as we make our way out of the house, and like the gentleman his mother swears he is, he opens the passenger door of his truck for me, waiting for me to climb inside before he walks around to get in behind the wheel.

"She heard our entire conversation," I hiss the second he closes the two of us inside the cab.

He chuckles. "The walls are thin."

I smack his arm with the back of my hand. "And you couldn't mention that? I'll never be able to face her again!"

His laughter continues as he rubs the spot on his arm like I frogged his muscle or something. "I thought you guessed that when she heard our conversation in the hallway."

"I wasn't thinking," I confess. "You have the ability to keep me from logical thought."

He cranks the truck as he looks over at me. "You get me all tied up too, McKenna."

I'd swoon at the sincerity in his voice if it wasn't for the shame I still feel for being so blazingly sexual where his mother could hear.

"She's never going to like me after that," I mutter as he pulls away from the curb.

"She already loves you. Plus, we're both adults, and you heard her. She remembers what it's like—" His sentence dies on his lips as a shudder wracks his body. "Can we change the subject?"

I laugh at his reaction even though I've been laughing at him most of the evening. He's a good sport, and that's an amazing quality to find in a man. What I haven't found, other than his initial cheesy pickup lines, are flaws.

"What's wrong with you?"

"Nothing. Why do you ask?"

"No, I mean, what are your flaws?"

He tilts his head as he pulls into the driveway at my duplex.

"Are you going to tell me you don't have any?"

He presses the button, killing the engine, and a thrill runs through me enough to make me forget my question. Is he planning to come inside? God, tell me he wants to come inside.

"I'm not perfect. Give me a second." His eyes look out the window as he thinks. "I'm possessive."

"Like violent?"

"Not really."

A hand scrapes over the stubble on his beard. This man could tell me he killed a guy that looked at his last girlfriend, and I'd just nod and smile, all the while wondering what those prickly hairs would feel like on my skin.

"I just don't want a woman I'm with flirting with other men."

"As they shouldn't."

His eyes find mine.

"You. I don't want you flirting with other men."

I grin at his seriousness. "Like the Tate brothers?"

He grins, knowing those guys don't have a snowball's chance in hell of getting my attention. "I'd punch both of them in the throat on principle and because I never got the chance when I found out they copped a feel of Kristina in high school."

"What else?"

"How many flaws do I need?"

"More than one."

"I'm told I snore when I'm sick."

I tilt my head, rolling my eyes. "Everyone does. That's not a flaw. Dig deeper."

"I love morning sex."

"Also, not a flaw, but good to know."

"I can't cook bread. It always burns."

I sigh, accepting that I won't get anything real out of him.

"I'm the type of guy who always jumps two steps ahead." He

breaks eye contact with me to focus his gaze through the windshield. "Normally, I go straight for the sex."

I kind of suspected this of him from day one, but it sets me back a little to hear the truth from his own lips.

"I jump to the end, but never have any desire to fill in the middle. You know, the parts that contain the dating and teasing and laughter, everything that builds up to that final act, and once it happens—"

"You're done," I fill in.

He turns his head, eyes on me. "I don't want to miss the middle with you, McKenna. I love spending time with you, seeing you hanging out with my family. I want my friends to be jealous of us because we're that couple that can't keep their hands off each other."

"Yeah?" My heart fills to the very top before overflowing.

"Yeah. I want it all, and in the right order. I don't want to ruin it by going too fast, by skipping steps."

"Are you really this perfect?" His confession doesn't feel like a game, but it also does nothing for the throbs in my body desperate to jump a few steps ahead. I want it all, and I'm trying to convince myself that I shouldn't have *all* of it tonight.

"Does that mean you're on board?"

I smile as I reach for the door handle. "Yes."

"Wait, where are you going?"

"Inside." I hitch a thumb over my shoulder.

"What about my goodnight kiss?"

"If I kiss you, we're going to end up skipping those steps you were so adamant about taking."

His eyes drop to my mouth. "I'm capable of stopping. Aren't you?"

My head is shaking before he finishes his question.

"No?" I shake my head some more. "So, I'm responsible for both of us?"

"Up for the challenge?"

"Can we have some ground rules?" I agree with a nod. "No clothes coming off."

"Does that include hands under clothes?"

He groans, rolling his head against his seat.

"What? I need straightforward rules."

"No hands under clothes."

"But hands on top of clothes?"

"Why don't we just hold hands for tonight?"

"Okay. Go on."

"You can*not* unbuckle my jeans."

"Even if I think you're in danger?"

"Oh, I'm definitely in danger." Somehow I'm able to keep a studious gaze on his face rather than dropping my eyes to his lap. "No pulling your own clothes aside."

"Doesn't that go hand in hand with no taking clothes off?"

He swallows, his eyes going to the bare skin below the hem of my skirt.

"Your own." I give him a confused look. "You can't pull your panties to the side."

"Jesus, Kalen. I wasn't even considering it until you opened your damn mouth."

He groans again, and I think this is the best kind of torture.

"This is a bad idea." He leans over and presses a quick kiss to my cheek. "I'll see you tomorrow... in the daylight... when other people are around."

I chew on the corner of my bottom lip before cupping his face with one hand and lowering my mouth to his. A pained sounds leave his mouth when I pull away.

"Goodnight."

"I'd walk you to the door, but Mom would hear about my hard-on before I even made it to my house." He points at a fluttering curtain across the street.

I laugh as I climb out.

"McKenna," Kalen says before I can close the truck door. "Send me some sexy pictures to get me through the night."

"In your dreams," I say with a smile, but then I get inside, and as I'm standing in front of my bathroom mirror, I feel sexier than I ever have before in my life. That's Kalen's effect on me.

I strip down to my underwear, noticing that my matching bra and panties—what? Don't judge, I knew I was going to his mom's house today, and that increased the chances of seeing him. I'm not eager, I'm prepared—they cover more than the bikini I wore to Padre last summer.

Before I can change my mind, I snap a picture in the full-length mirror and send it to him.

It takes two long minutes before I get a response. The first being a drooling face emoji, and the second a text saying he nearly drove into the ditch staring at it while he was driving. The third is asking if he can turn back around so I can fix the problem I've caused in his jeans, promising that he can get there without breaking any of the rules he gave tonight.

I almost accept, knowing I'm right on edge where he's concerned as well, but I shoot him a goodnight text and jump into a very cold shower.

Chapter 16

Kalen

"You seem different."

"I'm just me," I tell Mac, unable to keep the grin off my face.

I nod at the waitress as she places the pizza on the table between my best friend and me.

"Nope," he says as he grabs for a slice, dropping it on his plate with a wince. We've been coming here all our lives, and he never remembers how hot the pies are delivered to the damn table. "You're smiling."

"I always smile," I argue, waiting another minute before reaching for my own slice.

"It's that girl, isn't it?"

"What girl?"

"That teacher."

I tilt my head with mock confusion, my smile growing even wider.

"You bagged the teacher?" Mac asks before lifting his slice to his mouth and hhffhhhff-ing the bite until it's cool enough to chew.

"Could you not?"

"What? I'm freaking starving."

"I'm used to your inability to wait on food, Mac, I mean don't talk about her like that."

"This is the second time you've gotten defensive where she's concerned. Must be serious."

"I really like her, man."

"You really liked Joy and you see where that ended, right?"

"Joy and McKenna have nothing in common," I remind him. "And Joy's happy. I'm not upset she found true love."

"You mean a man she could walk all over? I wouldn't call that love. Did you see the way she bossed him around at the bar?" My friend shudders. "If that's what marriage is like, then count me out. I don't want any part of it."

"If the dynamic works for them, it's not our place to judge."

His eyebrows hit his hairline. "Were you abducted by aliens?"

I ignore the question, opting instead to bring my pizza to my lips and blowing to cool it down faster.

"You being in love is weird."

I open my mouth to argue about my feelings for McKenna, but immediately snap it closed. It may be love. I'm obsessed with her. Hate spending time without her. Can't stop staring at the picture she sent last night. She's always in my thoughts, and each recollection makes me smile. If this is love, then I'm all over it and never want it to end.

"Gross," Mac mutters around another bite of food. "Is she why you haven't been around much?"

"Feeling left out?" I tease, glad my food is finally cool enough to shove in my mouth.

"No," he snaps with a little too much agitation for me to believe him. "I've been busy myself. Just not *getting* busy like you must be doing."

And there's that jealousy I told McKenna I wanted.

"I haven't been spending every minute with her."

Unfortunately, we both have to work and that takes most of our time. Also, we're going slow, and that wouldn't be possible if we were around each other constantly. The chemistry is too strong for us to keep our hands to ourselves.

"And we haven't… you know. We haven't done that yet."

"Having trouble sealing the deal?"

"We're taking things slow."

"This isn't high school, man. Slow is for teenagers and virgins." He leans closer, his eyes bright with intrigue. "Is she a virgin?"

"Why so many questions about my girl?"

A wide smile spreads the expanse of his face.

"Man, leave it to you to bag the only virgin in town old enough to drive."

He lifts his fist for me to bump it, and I stare down at it before taking another bite of my pizza.

McKenna isn't a virgin. She said as much during our back-and-forth yesterday while Mom was making dinner, but I won't tell him about her confession of not having much experience.

"Oh shit," he whispers, but when I look up, his eyes aren't on me. "Don't look."

Of course, I look, and regret it the second I do.

"That woman hates you."

I turn back around as fast as I can, but not before Beth sees me looking in her direction.

"She didn't hate me the other night," I mutter.

Mac chokes on a bite. "Wh-What? You went there again?"

"What? No!" I hiss loud enough to turn several gazes in our direction.

Knowing the drill, we both sit silently for a few minutes until we think there's a good chance people have stopped trying to listen long enough to go back to their own meals and conversations.

"You can't be in love and still hooking up with Beth, Kalen. It's wrong." His eyes continue to dart over my shoulder, but I refuse to look a second time.

"I haven't hooked up with Beth. We made out that one time in my truck, and she went psycho. I haven't looked at her since."

"Name calling isn't necessary." My interest would pique at him defending her if I didn't have a point to make.

"The other night at the bar she talked to me. She was flirty and awkward, but at least it was civil. I didn't leave the bar wondering if my tires were going to be slit." Beth has never done something so destructive, but that thought is always in the back of my mind. I feel in my gut that the woman is capable of that and more when pushed.

"Oh."

I crinkle my nose at the relief in his tone.

"Mac."

His pizza is suddenly the only thing he can focus on.

"Mac!" His eyes—filled with guilt—snap up to mine before darting away. "Tell me you didn't hook up with Beth."

"I didn't." He swallows.

"You liar," I accuse. "Really?"

His eyes dart over my shoulder again.

"It was one time," he mutters, head hanging between his shoulders.

"One time is all it takes."

He shrugs. "I thought I'd like the attention. Plus, you're always busy with McKenna."

We spend a lot of time texting, but we haven't gotten as much in-person time as I'd like, but that's not the point.

"You're a grown man. Find something to entertain yourself with."

"I did." A wicked grin spreads across his face.

I huff a laugh. I have so many damned questions.

"Beth? Really? And now she's obsessed with you? Sheriff Hodson won't give you a restraining order. Believe me, I know that for a fact."

"She won't talk to me."

I tilt my head. "Huh?"

"We did the deed in my truck, and after I took her home, she never called."

The rest of the meal is spent in awkward silence, and I hate that Kristina has today off from work. It means she'll be picking Justin up, and I'll miss my daily dose of McKenna.

Chapter 17

McKenna

"Very good, Sammy," I praise as I walk around the room. "I love the sun in the sky."

"It's an octopus," he clarifies.

I smile and nod, wondering in what world an octopus flies in the sky, but whatever. At least the kid is working instead of picking his nose. I'm going to call it a win. "It's lovely."

I bend at the waist to see what Justin is coloring, tilting my head to try to determine what the glob of black is on his paper. My bra strap falls, and I resist the urge to huff in irritation. This one doesn't fit well, and the strap has been slipping all day. I need to do laundry, but I've been putting it off because the washer in our little complex isn't working.

A trip to the local laundromat, Get the Funk Out of Here, is going to be required, and I've been avoiding that place because it's right across the street from Hippie Jones' store. I don't have any more room on my shelf, and I know he'll see me coming from a mile away.

"What's that?" I ask Justin, once again slipping the wayward bra strap under the capped sleeve of my blouse.

"It's a black hole."

Okay, that makes perfect sense. I point to a series of red dots on the same page. "And those?"

"Those are aliens." I grin, standing to move on to the next kid. "Are you having trouble?"

My hand freezes on my arm where of course the damned strap has fallen again.

"Just a little wardrobe malfunction," I tell him with a chuckle.

He tilts his little head to the side, his eyes raking over my torso, and I'm trying to prepare myself for whatever he has to say. I can only hope it isn't insanely inappropriate, but he is related to Kalen, so there's no telling what's going to come out of his mouth.

"I think the black one fit better."

I never, not in a million years, thought he'd say something like that. My hand freezes on the strap, fingers trembling with anxiety.

"Wh-what?"

"The black one. The one you're wearing in the picture Freddie has."

A weak smile is all I can manage as he tucks his head back down to finish coloring. The child busies himself with his coloring unaware that he just rocked my entire world with a few well-placed words.

I know the color drains from my face before I make it to the classroom's en suite bathroom, and the mirror confirms it. My cheeks are pale, eyes wide and mouth hanging open in pure shock.

I was already anxious about sending that picture, body and self-esteem issues aside, but to discover he shared such an image with a five-year-old child? This goes beyond anything I could've ever imagined.

Somehow, I manage to make it through the last hour of class without fainting, studiously avoiding Justin so he doesn't bring up the damn bra once again, praying the entire time that none of the other kids overheard and go home to tell their parents one of the kids in class has seen me in nothing but my underwear.

I can't face the pickup line. I don't think I'll ever be able to face Kalen again. I knew he bordered on inappropriate, but showing his five-year-old nephew the photo I sent is a hit I never saw coming. It's practically illegal, and I feel shame for Kalen's actions clear down to my soul. I'm not only going to be jobless when word of this gets back to the principal, but I'll also be labeled as some type of pervert, even though I shared the photo with a grown man. Tears burn the backs of my eyes as I wait in my classroom for the car pickup line to run its course so I can leave for the day.

I look over my classroom, wondering if I'll even be back tomorrow. I could easily get the call insisting that I never step foot in the door ever again.

I knew Justin had boundary issues. I knew he and Kalen were

close, the kid seeing his uncle as more of a good friend than an authority figure, but this... this goes too far.

Needing to do something other than focus on the end of my career, I go home long enough to grab my dirty laundry before heading to Get the Funk Out of Here. If I'm going to be packing my belongings, I'd rather do that with clean clothes.

Old Man Hinkle is in the corner, nose tucked into a crime thriller book when I enter the laundromat. He barely glances up over the top of the novel before lowering his eyes to continue reading. Most days I'd find his presence comforting, knowing he'll eventually strike up a conversation about the raccoon in the tree outside the post office, but today I'm happy he's otherwise entertained. If he spoke to me, showed me any form of kindness, I'd probably start sobbing.

As I separate laundry into three different machines, I wonder if the entire town is a façade. If their kind words and welcoming attitudes are actually a ploy to draw people in so they can tear them down and ruin them.

Sniffling as I drop quarters into the last machine, my phone dings with a text notification.

Praying it's Courtney, I close the washer's lid and pull it from my purse. It isn't Courtney. It's the devil himself, sending yet another meme with a very sexual innuendo.

I'm not the pervert here, but nothing will land on the golden boy's shoulders. His mother is the president of the Sisters of Liberty. He's a professor at the college. He's the town's most eligible bachelor. I'm the outsider, no matter how excited people have pretended to have me in their little town.

I ignore the text, too shaken up just seeing his name on my phone, and settle into one of the surprisingly comfortable chairs as I wait for my laundry to wash.

He doesn't stop, and I count five new text messages, each one an image borrowed from somewhere on the internet that he no doubt thinks is funny. Only I'm not laughing. I'm not entertained. I'm no longer under his spell. I don't plan to respond to him at all. I managed to ignore him before, and I can easily do that again. My only struggle will be when I see him again face-to-face. My fingers won't tremble as I try to resist touching him or dragging my hands through his sexy hair. No, I'll have to restrain myself from wrapping my hands around his throat and squeezing.

Then he sends an actual text.

Kalen: I'm still hard from the picture you sent last night. *wink emoji

And that damn emoji sends me over the edge.

Me: You're the lowest of low. I never should've sent that picture. Are you purposely trying to ruin my life? Was this a joke to you the entire time? I think it's appalling that you would manipulate me the way you have, but I guess this is on me. I knew with that stupid pickup line at the school when I first saw you that I could never trust a man like you, but I never thought you'd share such an intimate picture, one I trusted you to keep to yourself, with a five-year-old child. I'm disgusted.

Kalen: What? I didn't. I'd never. What are you talking about?

So, this is the tact he's going to take? I know he'd give me puppy dog eyes if he were standing in front of me, and it only adds fuel to an already raging fire. Denial may work for the other people around here. He may be able to fool every one of them, but I'm not buying what he's selling.

Me: Justin was very specific today, telling me that he thought my black bra fit me perfectly. Don't ever message me again. When you see me on the street, don't bother opening your mouth. When you pick Justin up from school, don't even look in my direction.

I feel pride in the strength it takes to send that text, but then he doesn't respond, doesn't try to explain further, doesn't argue.

How can he? He was wrong.

But why do I feel a little more broken as I close my eyes and listen to the machines wash my soiled laundry? If only I could wash my hands of this entire town as easily as I can the three loads of laundry.

Chapter 18

Kalen

I shook uncontrollably when I got news that my father had passed away. It's the only time I can recall my body having such a violent reaction to a horrible piece of news until today. Sitting in my office and reading the texts from McKenna, I begin to shake again. The tremble begins not in my extremities but in my chest, my spine tensing first before fear makes its way into my nervous system. Before long, my entire body is shivering as if I'm stuck out in the cold instead of my office at the college.

Grading papers for another hour was my plan, but I can't even think about anything else but her.

Never speak to her again? That's not even an option.

I can't remember if I locked my office door when I fly out of the math building and head to my truck. I don't remember a second of the drive across town, banging my fist on the steering wheel when I see that McKenna's car isn't parked outside of her tiny duplex.

I head straight home knowing Kristina and Justin will be there, doing my best to calm down before confronting a five-year-old about what he found while snooping.

I can't think of a single second between now and last night where he would've had access to my phone. I've had the thing practically glued to my hand, and I've spent an unhealthy amount of time memorizing that image. There's no way he saw it.

I miss closing the door to my truck when I climb out in front of my house, but I just don't have the time to worry about it as I race inside. Kristina is at the kitchen sink washing vegetables for dinner, but she's not my focus.

"Hey," she begins but I leave the room the second I don't see Justin. "Good to see you, too."

"Where is he?" I snap when I don't see my nephew in the living room.

"Upstairs in his room," she says, turning off the water and facing me. "What's going on?"

"I love the little shit, but that won't stop me from shaking him," I hiss, taking the stairs two at a time.

I don't bother knocking on the kid's bedroom door. He's five. He doesn't get privacy around here.

"What did you do?" I say, my voice low and steadier than I feel right now.

Justin looks up from his iPad, his smile slipping away the second he sees my face. Apparently, I'm horrible at hiding my emotions.

"I didn't start another fire at school, and Gena is the one who thought hiding all the orange crayons was a good idea!" Justin's eyes dart to his mother, hoping for sympathy.

"I don't care what you did at school." That's a lie. My world is crashing down around me because of what he did at school, but kids not being able to complete the rainbow because a color is missing doesn't concern me. "What did you say to McK—Ms. Kaiser at school today?"

His eyes dart from me to his mother and back to me again.

"Sh-she—" His eyes dart again, and I'm seconds away from shoving my sister out of the room so he'll only be able to focus on me. "I know it was the wind, but she really did look like a witch."

"What?" Kristina asks.

"Her hair!" He points to his own little head, eyes wide. "It was all over the place. She really looked like a witch!"

"What did you say about the picture, Justin?"

A slow smile spreads across his face.

"Picture?" my sister asks. "What picture?"

I can't look at my sister right now. If I did, I'd probably blame her for her son being such a nosy brat and looking at things he's not supposed to.

"I told her the black one fit better because the red one kept falling down her shoulder." He beams as if he's the most helpful little guy in the world, and I try to stay angry. Thinking about what McKenna looks like in a red bra right now won't get me anywhere but half-hard and still angry because I may never get to see her in it.

"What?" Kristina shoves my shoulder. "What is he talking about?"

"He went through my phone," I hiss. "He saw a picture that wasn't meant for anyone but me, and then the little brat told McKenna about it. The woman hates me now. She thinks I showed—"

"I didn't go through your phone!" Justin screams, then as if he isn't in trouble, he starts playing on his iPad again.

"You gave him your phone? Don't you use a lock code?"

I turn to my sister. "I have nothing to hide."

"It's a security measure. Not only for him but for anyone else trying to dig into your personal stuff."

"He doesn't know boundaries!" I argue. "He shouldn't mess with my things."

"Look!"

Kristina and I both turn our heads. Her hand covers her mouth, and I feel my soul slip out of my body because right there on Justin's iPad is the very same image McKenna sent to my phone.

"This here." Justin points to the strap on her shoulder. I memorized that thin strip of elastic. I imagined more than once in the last eighteen hours pulling it down with my teeth. "This part, but red, kept sliding down her shoulder. I told her this one fit better."

Kristina chokes as Justin looks from the picture back to her.

"You always tell me to be helpful. I was being helpful."

"Give me that," Kristina snaps before I can do it myself. With the iPad in her hands, she looks down at the image. "Wow, she looks amazing."

"She's perfect." I yank the iPad from her hands and glare down at the stupid thing. Then I back out of the single image, and my world just gets worse. Every image saved on my phone is an album on his iPad.

"Why do you like purple fruit so much, Freddie?"

I swallow, wanting to hide the iPad but feeling guilty because I've somehow managed to corrupt my young nephew without even knowing it. I swipe through the images, mostly memes I've found online, but each one of them is horrible and very sexual. There's no pornography, but the wording on some make me grateful that he can't read very well yet.

"What have you done?" my sister whispers over my shoulder. "What kind of person are you?"

"I'm—I'm—"

"A sicko."

The tremble begins again, the iPad nearly falling from my hands. I don't know what to focus on—the things this child has seen or the mistake I don't know if I'll be able to fix.

"I told you this thing was a bad idea."

"You sound like Mom," I mutter. "I put parental controls on it."

"But that doesn't keep him from seeing everything you see. Did you use your own sign-up information?"

She swipes through the iPad, alternating between gasping and glaring at me.

"Yeah. I mean, he's too young to have his own email account."

"But you linked them?"

"I must have, but I didn't know he could see what I see."

"My kid is going to need therapy, and you're going to be the one to pay for it. God, Kalen, how could you be so careless?"

"Other than that picture—"

"And all the eggplant memes—"

"I didn't know!" I scrape my hands over my head. "He never said anything about them being linked."

"You keep using my lives on *Buddy Bash*," my nephew says.

My face falls. Until I first saw McKenna at his school, I was addicted to that stupid game. I figured I downloaded it after one too many drinks at The Hairy Frog, but I realize now things don't just travel from my phone to his iPad but also in reverse. It makes sense now all the apps I erase that end up showing up again. I bought my phone used from Ronnie Tate after seeing it on our local social media marketplace. I just figured it was a glitch.

"So many eggplants," Kristina mutters, and I yank the iPad from her hands before she goes digging deeper into my life.

I'm not a pervert, but I'm a man and there's no telling what kind of stuff I've looked up on my phone since I got Justin this iPad for Christmas. If he needs therapy, I'll gladly pay it because I feel terrible.

"Where are you taking that?" Justin cries when I turn to leave. "Don't punish me for your mistakes!"

"I'll fix it," I say as I head out of the room. "Just go play outside until I can take care of it."

I hug the offensive thing to my chest.

"You're leaving?" I ignore my sister as I descend the stairs. "We're in the middle of a family crisis."

I turn to face her midway down. "McKenna thinks I purposely shared that picture with your son. She hates me now, never wants me to speak to her again."

She folds her arms over her chest, eyebrows raising. "I don't blame her. You should be more careful with—"

"I didn't know!"

"Still." She must read the look of utter devastation on my face correctly because her posture changes. "Just explain it to her. She'll understand."

My throat threatens to close as I walk out of the house. I'm not as hopeful as my sister seems to be. McKenna is livid, rightfully so, but I don't know if I'll be able to get her to listen to me long enough to explain.

The second I'm in my truck and backing out of the drive, I call my mom.

"Hello, dear."

"Mom, don't ask questions, but I need you to find out where

McKenna is right now."

"Whatever do you mean?" Mom asks, making me roll my eyes. "I'm not a psychic."

"Mom," I hiss. "It's important. Find her for me."

I hang up before she can argue further. That woman might as well be clairvoyant with how easily she's able to access information. I'm surprised she hasn't called me already to bite my head off for what's happened.

Another drive by McKenna's house reveals that she still isn't home. I have no luck at the school either.

Then my phone rings.

"Where is she?"

Mom sighs on the other end of the line.

"You know, if you asked her to live with you, she wouldn't be where she is."

Live with me? I'll be lucky if the woman is able to look at me without sneering at this point.

"Where?"

"Get the Funk Out of Here. See, the machines in that housing area she lives in are broken. The parts are on order, but there's a delay in shipping at the factory in Houston. I think Jason is lying like normal, but as it were, she can't do laundry—"

I hang up on her, something I'll pay dearly for later, but listening to my mother gossip about Jason Brecken being a liar because he once placed flyers in the tenants' mailboxes without having them properly mailed from the post office isn't something I can sit through right now.

Getting to my girl and explaining how I'm a complete idiot is the only thing I can focus on right now.

Chapter 19

McKenna

Don't cry. Don't cry. Don't cry.

As I repeat the two words over and over in my head, I feel the threat of tears burning my eyes. My nose tingles with my effort, fingers tapping on my leg as I wait for my laundry to dry.

I haven't gotten another text from Kalen, but more importantly, I haven't heard from the school either. I don't know how I'll walk into class tomorrow and face Justin Alexander, but at least I may get the opportunity to try. That's what I have to focus on right now. If I think about how I trusted Kalen with that picture and him ruining everything, I'll lose it. Old Man Hinkle is growing more and more suspicious with my silence. He spoke once when he pulled his dog blankets from the washer and moved them to the dryer, but I was short in my answers. He didn't prod about my terrible mood, but I can see he's gearing up to ask questions. The last damn thing I need is him gossiping at his morning coffee roundtable with the other older gentlemen in town about what Kalen has done.

Movement outside the huge laundromat window draws my attention, but before Kalen can climb out of his truck, I'm ten times more livid and ready for battle.

I don't confront him when he walks in. I can't even bear to look in his direction. The tears that have been threatening for the last hour press against the backs of my eyes, and I hate him a little more for being able to get such strong emotions from me. I've only known the man for a couple of weeks. We've shared a few kisses and texts, but somehow I feel more betrayed than that time a friend in high school hyped me up, convincing me I'd look amazing with bangs.

In an effort to keep ignoring him when my heart is pounding in my chest, praying there's a reasonable explanation, I pull my still-damp clothes from the dryer.

"McKenna."

I don't acknowledge him or the shaking in my hands when I feel his presence get closer.

"Are you the reason this poor girl is all tied up in knots?"

Now is not the time for Old Man Hinkle to get involved, but maybe he'll be enough of a distraction to Kalen that I can get my laundry done and out of here.

"Will you let me explain?" Kalen asks, ignoring the indignant old man.

Hoping he'd leave me alone was a pipe dream, I guess.

My damp laundry becomes instantly more interesting as I rush to fold shirts and sleepwear.

"It was a mistake."

I scoff. Of course, he thinks it's a mistake now that he's been caught. Maybe I wouldn't feel as bad if he showed that picture to his friends. He said he wanted them jealous of what we have, but his nephew? I shudder in disgust.

If he does that with Justin, what is he willing to show our children?

The thought hits me like a baseball bat to the chest.

Our children?

When did I go from wanting to date this man to considering spending a life with him raising a family? I haven't even seen the guy naked, and my head is already—I shake the offensive thing because I will not go there right now, or ever.

I sniffle, refusing to let my tears fall. Everything is ruined.

"I didn't know the accounts were linked. McKenna, you have to believe me. I'd never share something so personal with anyone, especially not my—"

"Nudes are always a bad idea. A couple years ago, I sent—"

"Can you not?" Kalen snaps, drawing my attention to find him glaring at Theodore Hinkle. "This isn't about you."

I want to grab his arm and tell him to hold off. If Old Man Hinkle has experience with this sort of thing, I'm a little grossed out, but also intrigued. He has to be at least seventy, if not older. Surely, he doesn't mean he sent someone nudes of himself.

The old man shrugs. "Just saying these things have a way of spiraling out of control. I never thought my picture would go viral, but if you look on Gussied Up Geezers, I'm on the front page."

My eyes widen. This dirty old man.

I hide my smile before Kalen can turn his attention back to me.

I'm looking down at my clothes, fingers tangled in the fabric as I listen to Hinkle grumble about being betrayed by a man he thought he could trust. "Online doctor my ass. I never did find out what that rash was."

I nearly choke on my own tongue, all the while reminding myself I'm angry and have been betrayed.

"I set it up with my own information," he says, stepping so close I can feel the heat of him.

I feel like I've missed part of the conversation. Either that or he's as flustered as I am and not able to articulate what he's wanting to say.

"Jesus," he hisses.

My eyes widen when I look down at his hands to find him holding a pair of my panties.

When did he start helping me with my laundry?

"Give me that!" I yank the black lace from his fingers, but his hands just find another pair.

I shouldn't feel a certain way seeing his hands touching my underwear, but my body is rarely in sync with my brain. Hence, the situation I'm in right now. I knew sending that picture was risky, and here I am suffering the consequences of my own actions.

"Will you listen to me? I need to explain. It's all a misunderstanding." He drops the panties, placing his hand on my forearm, preventing me from searching through the damp clothes for every pair of panties left so I can hide them from him. He lost the right to see my unmentionables when he betrayed me.

"Don't," I hiss, hating that his touch is warm and somehow comforting even when I'm so angry.

"I'm not just going to walk away because you're angry." His hands clutch my shoulders, turning me to face him, but I keep my eyes lowered. I refuse to be ensnared by him, and I know that's what will happen if I look him in the eyes. His finger hooks under my chin, and I see the devastation I'm feeling mirrored back from his handsome face. "I got Justin an iPad for Christmas. When I set it up, I used my account information. I should've known it was too easy since I nearly went insane setting up my phone. I linked the accounts."

I already know where this is going, and it makes sense, but I let him keep talking. He'll mess up and lie at some point. I just know it. There's no way this was a simple mistake. There's no way I overreacted without considering all the possibilities. I'm a logical person, but Kalen has had my head jumbled for weeks.

"I didn't know that everything I save on my phone also saves on his device." His eyes plead with mine. "I didn't show him the picture. The thought of that is absolutely disgusting, honestly, but he did see it because I saved it. Maybe I shouldn't have, but God, you looked amazing. I'd never—"

"Enough." His face falls. "I believe your explanation, but—"

"Oh, thank God. I'd never—"

"But," I repeat. "It doesn't change the fact that one of my students has seen me half-naked."

"It's not a big deal."

If I could shoot lasers out of my eyes at this man, I'd do it with glee.

"Not a big deal?" I step back, watching as his hands fall helplessly to his sides. "I could lose my job, Kalen. I know I may not have a renewed contract for next year, but this could ruin my chances of getting a job anywhere else."

"He won't tell anyone."

"He blurted it out in the middle of class. I'm surprised I haven't gotten a *you're fired* call from the principal already."

"If it comes to that, I'll make sure to speak with Deena. She loves me."

I narrow my eyes at him, but I wouldn't be surprised to find out it's true. The jerk is insanely charming.

"I'll have a long conversation with Justin. He won't mention it again."

I shake my head. I was so ready to hate him, to walk away—albeit brokenhearted—and never look back. My body doesn't know how to handle this new information.

"Please, McKenna. You have to know that I'd never do anything to mess up what we have." His eyes search mine, darting between them like he's searching for clues that I still care or am willing to give him a second chance. "I think I'm fall—"

"Stop!" I hiss, reacting like a crazy person and using my fingers to clamp his lips closed.

He mumbles around the pinch, but thankfully the words are indecipherable.

With a gentle hand, he pulls my fingers from his face, kissing my palm before tangling our fingers. "I'll do anything to make it up to you. Absolutely anything."

I blink up at him, relief washing over me like a tidal wave. The force of it threatens to sweep me off my feet.

"Linked accounts?" He nods, fingers holding my hand tighter. "I'm still mad."

"I know." He takes a step closer. "I swear it was a mistake. Tell me what you need to make it better."

I don't ask for a thing. If he's going to talk to Justin and make him understand this isn't something to spread around town, then that's enough for me. It still doesn't dismiss the fact that I probably won't be around this time next year. There's no telling where my next teaching job will be, but I decide to live in this moment while I have it.

"You owe me big time."

A slow smile tugs up the corners of his mouth, but he clears his throat as if he's thinking things he doesn't feel he has the right to imagine. Just the prospect heats my body.

"Anything," he whispers before lowering his face and brushing his warm lips against mine.

I let it happen. Hell, I want more, but we're in public, and I've already been too vulnerable in public enough today. I take a step back, unlinking our hands and gathering the rest of my laundry.

"I'll never send you another picture like that."

His face falls, but he looks resolved.

"I know."

"I want you to delete that one." You'd think I was the one to tell him Santa isn't real with the pain in his eyes. "From all devices."

"Okay." The kicked puppy look really does work for this man.

"You know—" We both turn to see Old Man Hinkle with his head poked through the front door of the laundromat. "It can't be all that bad. Just show me the picture, and I'll let you know."

I'm smiling when Kalen growls at him, but I'm able to catch his arm and hold him back before he's able to make good on his threats.

Chapter 20
Kalen

"This is bullsh—" I snap my mouth closed, smiling at the little girl walking a poodle instead of letting loose a string of profanities. "Are you having fun?"

The little girl looks from my face to the bucket hanging loosely from my fingers and scrunches up her freckled little nose. Then she takes off running like I'm planning to throw dog feces on her.

I told McKenna I'd do anything to gain her forgiveness, and I meant it. What I didn't anticipate is being the sole person responsible for keeping the park clean during *Pets and Pinot*, a yearly event held in Lindell where pet owners come out to mingle all while getting drunk on vendor samples of wine.

The event is a hit every year, one I've actively participated in even though I don't have a dog because... free booze.

This year is different, and I have a renewed respect for the person who had this job every year prior.

I flex the handle of the poop scooper, urging the latest pile to fall in the bucket and move on to the next. Some of these dogs need a different diet because I'm left gagging more than once.

I don't blame McKenna for being stuck with this shitty job. This has my mother written all over it. Rebecca Shears guilted McKenna into helping, persuading her with the promise of puppy cuddles and the best red wine she's ever tasted. It was a test of my mother's, a chance to see if McKenna was going to back out once she realized the teen scheduled to do this job was conveniently out of town. Ruptured appendix, my ass. I don't care if he posted pictures from a hospital bed. Kids are crazy good with Photoshop these days.

McKenna would've done this job with a smile on her face, but that smile has been even wider every time I see her looking over at me. I'm not a happy man doing this, but seeing the satisfaction on her face that I said I'd do it without arguing is worth every clump of crap I'm going to pick up today.

I stand in the middle of the field watching as Sheriff Hodson chases after a frisky chihuahua with its sights set on a huge bulldog. With a water bottle in hand, he sprays the dog time and time again, but the tiny thing isn't deterred.

"I understand you more than you'll ever know, buddy," I grumble.

McKenna and I have spent time together since our conversation at Get the Funk Out of Here, but holding hands is as far as things have gone. I want to kiss her. I know she wants to kiss me if I'm going by the way she continuously stares at my mouth when I'm talking, but we haven't crossed that line again. I haven't had my lips on her since the brief kiss after I begged for her forgiveness, and I'm dying to get her alone. But I need her to know she's more than a way to get my rocks off. She means more to me than any woman ever has, and as painful as it is to take things slow, I'll move at the speed of a glacier if it means we end up together.

"That is the best kind of torture." I nearly pant as I watch McKenna bend over to scratch under the chin of a wiggly puppy.

I'd be just as damn giddy if she were touching me like that. Does she realize how far her flowy skirt rides up when she bends like that? Is it wrong to wish for a stiff breeze?

My eyes scan the area, knowing I'll kill any man I find looking in her direction. Thankfully, my criminal record stays clean and my good grace with the small community remains intact when I see everyone in attendance is busy chatting and playing with their dogs.

With a moment of rallied strength, I glance around the field to find it free of piles and instantly make my way across the park to her. I don't interrupt her moment with the ecstatic puppy, and I also don't pull my eyes from the expanse of tanned legs exposed by her posture either. I'm probably in love with this girl, so it doesn't feel like a violation.

"Creep." I grin at the sound of my best friend's voice.

"Hey, man. Where are you going?" I watch as Mac walks right past me, but then I follow the point of his finger to see Beth. She doesn't look happy, and I know she saw me looking at McKenna with open desire in my eyes. The woman is going to have to get over it eventually. We were never a thing, and we will never be a thing. I grin, watching Mac approach her, and refocus on my girl.

Only she's no longer bending over but standing directly in front of me.

"She hates you," she says after looking in the direction I just pulled my eyes from. "And Marcy hates you, too. Should I be worried that all your past girlfriends despise you?"

I smile down at her, but not because of the faux concern in her voice. I grin because she is the most beautiful woman I've ever laid eyes on and also because her own eyes are a little glazed over, and her cheeks are pink.

"Have you been sampling from the vendors?" I run the back of my hand down her flawless cheek.

"I didn't realize there would be over two dozen vendors here."

"You're in wine country." I trace my finger along her shoulder because I can't be this close to her and not touch her. "Are you saying you sampled every one of them?"

Her grin is contagious.

"No." She smacks my chest, but her movements are slow enough that I'm able to catch her hand and hold it against my shirt. I wonder if she can feel how much it makes my heart rate spike? "I stopped after three booths, but I did try three different wines at one place. I've never even heard of Tiger Milk, and it's a weird name, but the taste was—"

"Tiger Milk? You had three glasses at Luther McDonald's booth?"

She chuckles before covering her mouth when it turns into an adorable snorting sound. "He said he had a farm."

Her laugh grows.

"Get it? Old McDonald's farm?"

I wait for her to calm down, and let's just say it takes a few moments. I bask in her presence, grinning right along as she laughs.

"Luther doesn't make wine, McKenna." Her head snaps back like she's been poisoned. "Tiger Milk is moonshine."

Her lips roll between her teeth, but her jovial mood is back and shining brightly behind her eyes. "Moonshine?"

"Did you like it?"

She leans in close. "I bought two full bottles. It was the best tasting stuff, even with that extra zingy kick that made my spine roll up on itself."

"Have you forgiven me?" I ask out of the blue, not wanting to ruin her good mood, but also no longer able to wait.

I could just forget the fight happened, but it had the power to nearly ruin what we were building together. I want to put it behind us as soon as possible.

She snorts for a second. "Have you picked up all the doggy bombs?"

"I have."

"Then I forgive you." I lean my head down to kiss her, but she pulls her head back. "If your nephew brings it up again, the fight will start all over."

That child better not utter another word. The brat saw the opportunity and used it to bribe me out of a hundred bucks. Part of me was proud he saw the chance to make some money, but the other part of me wanted to shake him until he agreed. Since I'm not a violent person, and child abuse is illegal, we settled on a hundred bucks and letting him stay up late to watch *Mickey Mouse Clubhouse*.

Speaking of mystery mouseketools...

"Will you take a walk with me?"

Her hand flies to her chest in mock disbelief. "What will the townsfolk think if I'm seen walking around in the dark with such a rakishly handsome man?"

I give her a cheesy wink before grabbing her hand and dragging her across the park.

Chapter 21
McKenna

"These are amazing." I groan around yet another bite of taco. "Almost good enough to forget we got them from a guy with a food truck called The Pink Taco."

Kalen laughs, and it's hard not to focus on the spot of sour cream at the corner of his mouth.

"Wait until the Lindell Jubilee. We have over twenty food trucks that show up, and each one of them has an equally funny name."

My eyes light up. "Any Thai food?"

God, I love Thai food, and there isn't a place in town that sells anything like what I could get in Dallas.

"I don't know if Pretty Thai for a White Guy will make it this year. He flirted with Old Man Hinkle's granddaughter last year, and the old fogey wasn't very impressed."

I laugh at that. I can see Theodore holding his fists up, age spots and all, and threatening to kick the out-of-towner's butt.

"This is nice," I tell Kalen as I crinkle up the paper on my final taco.

"There's no one else in the world I'd rather eat pink tacos with."

He winks, and I feel a blush cover my cheeks. The man is full of innuendo, although he has kept things very PG lately. I don't know if he's trying to be chivalrous or if he's honestly afraid to make a move since our argument.

"Wanna go for a walk?" He stands, holding out his hand.

As a joke, I drop my trash in it rather than give him my own hand, but he takes it in stride, walking the trash to the receptacle before coming back and holding out his hand again. This time I take it, letting our fingers tangle together so perfectly it's like they were made to be the other's counterpart.

Without hesitation, I lean into him as we walk. The sun has set further, leaving nothing around us but the sound of crickets and the soft glow from the town's old-school streetlamps. It's romantic without even trying, and I know why so many people around here choose this place to spend hours of their time.

We don't speak as we walk. We just take in the sights of people in the distance with their dogs. They're happy, all smiling and talking to each other like family. Only a few kids remain, chasing around dogs who eagerly soak up the attention with tails wagging and an occasional yip of excitement.

"You don't have a dog?" I ask when I really want to find out if he wants children. That conversation may be a little premature, and the last thing I want to do is scare this man off. I've pushed my imminent departure from my mind, opting instead to focus on the here and now, needing every ounce of joy I can find before having to say goodbye.

"I don't," he answers. "Do you like dogs?"

"Love them. I had a dog growing up, but he passed when I was a sophomore in college. I was heartbroken."

"I can imagine. We never had animals growing up. I'm allergic to cats, so I think Mom was always afraid I'd be allergic to dogs despite me playing with my friends' dogs and never having a reaction. Wanna sit?"

I follow the point of his finger to a huge tree near the edge of the park. The *Pets and Pinot* participants are far enough away now that even their laughter barely makes it to us on the breeze.

"Sure."

Kalen sits down on the ground, uncaring if he gets his clothes dirty, and I take a place directly beside him, the warmth of his thigh making me all too aware that we're truly alone right now. My heart pounds, pulse so loud in my ears that I feel silly for having such a visceral reaction to touching legs.

"Did you like growing up here?"

"Loved it," he answers without hesitation. "I think I wanted to get away when I was a teen. As you've found out, there are no secrets in this town, but I came back the second I graduated undergrad. Teaching at the school was a challenge because I wasn't used to being around children, but then Justin was born, and it just became second nature."

"You taught at my school?" I can't picture him as an elementary teacher at all.

"Two years as the high school math teacher. I've been at the college now for a year and a half."

"Those poor high school girls." His brows furrow. "Really?"

"What?"

"Did you ever have a moment's peace? I imagine there was always some poor girl needing help with her classes."

"Math is hard for many people."

I scoff. "And it didn't hurt that the teacher was smoking hot either."

His smile is wide as his teeth dig into his lower lip. "You think I'm hot?"

I smack him, but he catches my hand.

"I bet it's the same way at the college."

"Are you jealous?" he asks, using his grip on my arm to pull me closer.

"Of college girls? *Should* I be worried about college girls?" He shakes his head. "Then maybe I am a little jealous they get to see you more often than I do."

"I can wait around after picking Justin up and take you home every day if you want."

"You want to spend time with me every day?"

He nods, his eyes focused on my lips. "Every second of every day."

"Sounds a little excessive," I manage as he leans in closer.

"Obsessive," he corrects. "As in obsessed... with you."

Our lips meet, and even though it's been days since we really kissed—I'm not counting the apology kiss at the laundromat—he doesn't just dive in. Each brush is a tease. Each nip at my lower lip is a promise of what he could be doing.

He drives me mad, so incredibly out of my mind that I don't even realize I've straddled his legs until his strong hands are gripping my butt.

"McKenna," he pants against my mouth. "You drive me wild."

Then he's kissing me for real, his mouth skating over mine, tongue begging and immediately gaining entrance to my mouth. His breaths escape his nose in harsh exhales, mixing with panty-melting groans when I shift my weight on him.

"So perfect. God, roll your hips like that again."

I do, feeling the rush of desire that has no place in such a public setting with people who would judge us for getting frisky less than a hundred yards away. Even if we weren't blocked by the huge tree at our back, I can't stop the movement of my body. I'm being controlled by under-sexed desire right now.

I squeal when a spray of water hits my back, and again louder when I turn my face only to be met with another spray of water.

I'm off his lap and falling to the ground beside him in less than a second, shielding my face and trying to figure out what the hell is going on.

"Dammit, Mike. Would you stop that?"

"It's Sheriff Hodson, son. You'd do well to remember that. Haven't you learned your lesson about fornicating in the park?"

I freeze, but I don't know if it's because the sheriff is standing in front of us with a spray bottle or if it's his reference to Kalen doing this more than once. I haven't heard stories about his escapades, and other than seeing women fawn over him at the bar, I haven't seen him flirting with anyone.

"Fornicating? I wasn't," Kalen argues. "Making out with my girlfriend isn't illegal."

"Would your momma approve?"

"She loves McKenna."

"Would she love knowing her son is getting freaky in the park?"

"We were kissing."

I'm so embarrassed, I hang my head and bury my nose in Kalen's shoulder.

"Practically humping," he corrects accurately, and it serves to bring on more shame. "And you said the same thing when I caught you down here with Beth Meyer. That poor brokenhearted girl. The wedding never happened, and I still haven't gotten those fancy wooden salad bowls back."

I stiffen. I haven't known him long enough to get a full life story, but I sat for hours going through photo albums with his mother. Certainly, she would bring up a failed engagement, right?

I don't feel like I've been lied to, but I do feel like I've been left in the dark. Kalen must sense my uneasiness because he shifts his weight, lifting my chin much the same way he did earlier this week after the picture debacle.

"We weren't married. I made out with her—kissing, no wandering hands—once. The girl took that as a marriage proposal. She's a little nuts."

"She's a fine young woman," Sheriff Hodson interrupts.

"She's certifiable. We weren't engaged, but she somehow convinced people around town we were. I promise."

"I want those bowls back," Sheriff Hodson insists.

"You'll have to talk to Beth," Kalen snaps.

A smile spreads across my face when Kalen grins at me, and once again I feel trapped in his orbit. Eventually, I hope to learn to ask questions rather than jumping to conclusions because nothing around this town is ever as it seems from the outside looking in. Assumptions got me in trouble once, and although I vowed to never let it happen again, I was seconds away from getting up and leaving Kalen sitting in the park.

"Don't worry, Sheriff Hodson." I turn my attention away from Kalen. "I'm in no danger of falling under this man's spell."

Kalen tenses beside me, and as I stand, swiping leaves and debris from my clothes, I let him suffer with thinking I'm walking away. Call it a little punishment for the discomfort he's caused me on more than one occasion.

"Very good, young lady. I knew you had a smart head on your shoulders."

"In fact," I say, turning my head to wink at Kalen. "I must insist that he take me home immediately. What would my mother say if she discovered that I had a weak moment being charmed by such a lothario?"

"My apologies, Ms. Kaiser," Kalen says, catching on rather quickly.

"I can escort you," Sheriff Hodson urges. "There's no telling what he'll try between here and your home."

My face falls. How can I argue with the man?

"Nonsense," Kalen says, climbing to his feet and standing between Sheriff Hodson and me. "I'll see that she makes it safely."

Before Hodson can argue, Kalen hooks his arm in mine and drags me away. When I begin to laugh, I pray I'm far enough away that he can't hear it.

"You're bad," Kalen says as we walk along the sidewalk to my house.

"What else was I supposed to do? Getting caught in the park alone, dry humping the town's Casanova? My reputation would be ruined. Poor Beth Meyer."

"One, you could've defended me."

"While you were trying to steal my honor?"

He huffs. "You were assaulting me if I recall correctly. And two, poor Beth Meyer?"

"She's a little obsessed with you."

"She mostly just gives me evil looks, but she was one of the women talking to me that night in the bar when you were there with your friend. She didn't seem to hate me then."

"I completely understand your appeal when I've been drinking, so I can see how she'd be more receptive to you if she had been drinking."

I yip in surprise when he swings me around, my back pressing gently against a tree. "Is that why you were all over me in the park, because you've been drinking?"

"I'm completely sober. Those tacos worked wonders."

His lips are mere inches from mine, but he doesn't close the distance. "I like what we did at the park."

"I did, too," I whisper. "Let's go back to my place where we can do it without getting sprayed with water like two humping dogs."

Chapter 22
Kalen

"I had a great time today," I say against McKenna's lips as we stand on her front porch. "Even if I had to pick up dog poop for three hours."

"I'm glad you were there to help."

I press my mouth to hers one more time, trying my best to ignore the way her fingers are tangled in my shirt.

"I'll see you tomorrow?" God, please don't make her put distance between us overnight.

"Tomorrow?" She grins, her eyes a little unfocused and zeroed in on my mouth. "Like when you get up and make me breakfast?"

Is she suggesting...?

Then she makes it very clear, grabbing a belt loop on my jeans and dragging me inside her little house.

She's a woman crazed as she presses my back to the front door, making it snap closed. We had rules, and she breaks one of them as she lifts my shirt, her fingernails scraping over my torso. My body flexes, muscles growing tight and begging for more as her mouth angles over mine.

"McKenna," I growl when her fingers fumble with the top snap of my jeans. "We're getting very close to the point where we can't turn back."

"I passed that point in the park," she whispers against my lips before nipping at my jaw. "You're going to need to be the one to pump the brakes."

"The lines are cut, and we're rolling down a hill," I mutter, turning my head when her soft, warm lips meet the column of my throat. Did she just nip at my Adam's apple? Damn, why is that so hot? "Do you want to stop?"

My chest is heaving as she pulls back, and I'm praying I can hide the disappointment I know I'm going to feel when she says yes.

"No," she says instead, and the single word ignites my entire body, even the parts of me that have been holding back, waiting for the perfect moment.

This is it. This is the right time, the right place. Jesus, I feel like I've known her my entire life, as if I've been pining for her for years and she's just now giving me the nod of approval, as if I have one shot to get it right.

My eyes begin to flutter when she steps into me again, but then something darts, catching the corner of my eye across the room.

"You have a mouse!" It scuttles again. "No! It's a rat. The thing is huge!"

Forget my man card. Forget being a hero and saving her from another plague. It's every man for himself. I squeal like a preteen meeting a Jonas brother and haul ass across the room, jumping on the couch. I spin in a circle trying to get a lead on the damn thing so I can be prepared if it tries to climb my leg and chew my face off.

"Really?" I look across the room to see McKenna standing with both fists on her hips, much the same way she was when we first met, and just like then, she's watching me with equally unimpressed eyes.

"Get up here!" I wave her over, praying she makes it without getting attacked because I'm no hero right now. Rats? Any form of rodent? Hard freaking pass, this time and every other time until the end of time.

I barely hide the shudder as tingles crawl up my spine. Some people are frightened of spiders and snakes, both reasonable phobias. It just so happens that goats and rats have the ability to put the fear of God in me. People really shouldn't judge.

"I don't have rats."

"I saw it with my own eyes."

She sighs. "Not a rat. Get down from there."

"I won't." I give my head an emphatic shake, trying to hold her eyes, but needing to look around for danger. "Come here. I'll hold you until it's safe."

The damn thing runs right out into the open, and instead of her shrieking like any sane person would, she squats and picks the vile thing up in her hands. Everything I know and love about this woman shatters right before my eyes, and I would sob at my loss if my mouth wasn't hanging open when she brings the thing under her chin and begins to coo at it.

"This is Garrett."

"Hard pass!" I yell, much louder than I intended to. No doubt I just rattled pictures on the neighbor's walls, but holy hell. A rat cuddler? Nope. Not even love is strong enough for that mess.

"He's a ferret, not a rat."

The creature turns its white head, using beady red eyes to threaten me.

"Ferrets have tails."

"He's supposed to have a tail, too," she argues, making me snap my jaw closed. "He was a rescue. His previous owners didn't pay attention when they closed doors."

Her explanation doesn't calm me completely, but I do feel safe enough to get my dirty damn shoes off her sofa.

"Ferrets aren't solid white."

"Albino ones are. Come pet him."

"I love you, McKenna, but I'm not petting a rodent."

I know ferrets aren't rodents, but I have a point to make, and I must make it very clear because her eyes snap up to mine. Without another word, she pets the vile creature on the head as she walks across the room. A moment later, she's placing it gently into a cage and locking the thing away. My heart rate immediately begins to slow, only to ratchet back up when she refocuses on me as she begins to draw closer.

"What did you say?"

"I won't pet it." When her eyes narrow, I backpedal a little. Why can't she understand? Maybe she's never been bitten by a rodent, but I have. I'd have the same reaction if she pulled out an evil little hamster or guinea pig. "I'm not comfortable petting it *tonight*. Maybe it'll grow on me, but I just can't touch it righ—"

"Before that, Kalen."

I try to run through the catalog of things I've said, but only the less than manly screams and fear come to mind.

"Wow," I say once again distracted.

I walk past her, unwilling to talk about my little freak-out. Maybe distracting her will help. I know what I want to do, but my body is going to take a little time to catch up with my freaked-out brain.

"Hippie Jones is worse than a used car salesman," McKenna says as I walk up to the wall of bongs.

"Does Deena know you're into this stuff?"

She huffs a laugh. "They're handmade works of art."

Even I'm not convinced with her argument. I pick up a pink and purple glass bong, rolling it around in my hand until I find the sticker on the bottom. I hold it up to show her.

"That dirty bastard. Do you know what I paid for that?" She glares like I'm guilty by association. "Made in China? He has an entire story about each one of these pieces."

She waves a hand to indicate the more than three dozen different sized bongs on display in her living room.

"That one he made from sand he collected when he was backpacking in Nepal."

"Stanley has never been outside of the United States."

Her eyes widen again. "Lies. It's all lies. This whole town is lies. You're a liar!"

"Me?" I don't waste time shoving the bong back on the shelf and pressing my body against hers. "I didn't lie to you."

"And you wouldn't answer my question either."

"I'm an open book, McKenna."

"What you said earlier?"

My heart pounds because on my trek across the room, I realized what she was asking me to repeat.

"That I love you?" I swallow thickly. "I do, so freaking much."

She gasps.

"Is it too soon?"

Her mouth opens and closes like that time Mac's goldfish did when it kept jumping out of its water bowl.

I press my finger to her chin, urging her mouth closed.

"I love you, McKenna Kaiser."

And then we kiss. When my lips meet hers, the devil creature across the room disappears, the world stops, and my new life begins. Kissing for the first time after saying those words is transformative. It's a slice of heaven right on earth. Right in the middle of Lindell, my world narrows to just her and me.

Both of our hands flutter, items of clothing getting pulled away and discarded. Nothing can ruin this moment. Not Satan screeching from its cage or stubbing my toe on the wall as we try to make it to her room with our mouths locked together. Not her light bulb popping and casting us back into darkness when I hit it as I pull my shirt over my head. The car alarm going off down the street doesn't even have the power to pull my attention from this woman.

I need inside of her, need to taste every inch of her body, but then the glow from the streetlight outside catches in her hair. I see her standing in the middle of her room in nothing but her bra and panties, the same set she was wearing in the picture that nearly had the power to end us before we even really started.

"You are positively gorgeous."

"Yeah?" she whispers, her hands folding behind her back.

Things only get better from there. Her bra flutters to her feet as her fingers dip into the lace at her hips, and when those fall to the ground, I'm frozen in place, torn between devouring her and just staring at her perfection for the rest of eternity.

"Feel like sharing?"

I don't realize until she speaks that my hand is stroking up and down my cock over my boxers.

"This?" I shove my boxers to the floor, pretending I don't stumble as they tangle around my feet before I can fully step out of them. "This is all yours."

She squeals when I pick her up, but then her legs wrap around my waist, the heat of her pressing in all the right places.

I'm lost once again, tangled up in her as we fall to her bed.

"I don't have a condom," I hiss when she rolls her hips like she did at the park, but this time there's absolutely nothing between us. The friction is enough to make my eyes roll into the back of my head.

"I do," she says, pointing to her bedside table.

I look down at her with narrowed eyes. "You planned this?"

A slow seductive smile spreads across her face. "Do you think the matching bra and panties were pure luck?"

She smacks my chest in a *you silly boy* kind of way. "Get the condom. I'm not on birth control. What would your mother say if you got me pregnant?"

"About time. I've always wanted more grandchildren."

"Really?" The smile never leaves her face.

"Yeah," I tell her honestly, curving my back so I'm lined up just perfectly. "What do you think?"

I press forward, the tip of me sliding easily through her desire, but the heat that grips me makes my mind up for me.

She whimpers in need, a sound that threatens to end this too soon, when I pull away.

"I promised you before I was an expert at sex, but I get the feeling you'll make fun of me if we do this the first time without something that dulls the sensation a little."

I reach for the condoms and groan at the package.

"I shouldn't have gotten ultra-thin then. Huh?"

"You can't judge me."

"Never," she assures me, and when she runs her palm up and down my arm as I wrap up, I wonder if she uses that same tone with her kids at school when they get upset over something.

"Baby," I hiss, lining myself up again and dipping the tip right back where it was. There's no damn difference. The heat is the same. The grip is the same. The only difference is—"Please, don't," I beg when she rolls her hips.

"Might as well get it over with."

"Over with? I don't want to get it over with." I press closer to her, but the second my nuts seize, I pull all the way out. "You first."

And then my mouth is on her, trailing down her neck, over her breastbone, only taking quick seconds to lap the tips of her perfect tits. I'm a man on a mission, and if she thinks I don't have every intention of keeping her up all night, then she should've grabbed the three-pack of condoms instead of the twelve.

Her laughter dies on her lips when I form a suction around her most sensitive parts. My tongue works overtime, and less than five minutes later, she's leaving a bald spot on my head, so overcome with sensation that I leave her whimpering.

"Please," she begs when I nip at the spot just below her belly button.

"You just begged me to stop."

"I shouldn't have to beg at all."

Her hands are stronger than she lets on when she tugs me up her body, and as if I've always lived inside of her, our bodies line up perfectly. Her mouth is on mine when I push into her, and this time she's the one swallowing my pleas. My skin feels like it's on fire. My heart pounds, and this is so much more than a sexual experience. I want to bury my head in the crook of her neck and hide, but at the same time I want her to know exactly what this means to me.

Her hand cups my jaw when I look down at her.

Words.

I have so many to say. So many things I want her to know, but I'm just not capable.

My muscles tense, my spine tingles, and a low burn starts in my lower abdomen.

"I love you, too," she says, the words so soft and sweet they cling to me as I explode.

I can't blink, can't even look away.

"Love you," I pant.

I hold myself off of her, not wanting to crush her but still unable to pull free. I wasn't lying when I said I wanted this every second of every day. Now that I've had a taste, we may never step foot outside again.

"I don't want you to freak out."

"Nothing good ever comes from starting a sentence like that," I whisper, nuzzling my nose along her throat.

She runs her warm foot up the length of my calf, and it calms me. I can handle whatever it is she has to tell me if she keeps comforting me like this.

"What? Mmm, I like you rubbing my leg like that."

"That's Garrett. He's a little escape artist."

I don't think I've ever moved so fast in my life. I'd blame the shriek as I throw the covers back and scramble out of the bed on the cold air hitting my man parts, but we both know better.

"I've been betrayed!" I yell as I sprint across the room to the bathroom.

Her laughter follows me inside, and I don't know how to feel when I hear her cooing to the gross little thing when I climb in the shower.

Chapter 23
McKenna

My eyes dart everywhere and I'm sure I've never seen so much purple before in my life.

"Amazing isn't it?" I grin over at Kalen.

We're in the stands of the Lindell University basketball arena for an end-of-the-year pep rally. The school is massive, the campus probably bigger than the rest of the town.

"Lindell is known for its athletes."

I look around the room, knowing he must be telling the truth because there's a lot of money that has gone into the school, and I doubt Mrs. Shears and the others in the small town can hold enough fundraisers to provide such commodities to the school alone.

"Seriously," he says as if he thinks I don't believe him. "Ever heard of Jace Gentry?"

"The quarterback for the Pittsburg Dingoes?"

He nods. "Graduated from here. Was drafted between his junior and senior year, and he's one of over a hundred that walked the halls of this school before making it to the big leagues."

"That's amazing."

He looks down at me smiling, but the twinkle in his eyes speaks more to what he wants to do with me after we leave than what he's actually saying.

We've been inseparable the last couple of weeks, and although he's always on edge where Garrett is concerned, he's never once turned down my offer to stay over. His house isn't an option. He claims I'm too loud and answering the questions it would raise for Justin isn't something he's going to do. He still gets up and takes him to school, and picks him up when Kristina is working, but any spare minutes we have, we spend them together. It's been absolute bliss.

"Is this spot taken?" I look up to see Oakleigh standing near us, pointing to the empty spot in front of us.

"Please."

"You know her?" Kalen hisses in my ear only loud enough for me to hear.

"Do you?" I say, trying to keep my nerves calm.

I've never been the type of woman to get jealous, but Oakleigh is a very pretty girl.

"She's in my class, but my cousin Collins is in love with her."

"The one that goes to college here?"

He nods. "She won't give him the time of day. It's been fun to watch this year."

"I didn't know a woman existed that could resist an Alexander man."

His smile widens as he presses a swift kiss to my lips. "You make my heart smile, McKenna Kaiser."

"Same, Kalen Alexander."

"Have you ever—oh, sorry."

I smile against Kalen's lips before turning my attention to Oakleigh. Her eyes dart away, her cheeks flushed. If I had to guess, I'd say she's either embarrassed to find us kissing or because she got caught staring.

"What were you asking?" I swat at Kalen's hands when he tries to turn my face in his direction again.

I love kissing the man. I love everything about him, but he has issues controlling his body no matter where we are. I won't even go into what happened last week in the back booth at the Brew and Chew, but I know I won't be able to look Ruth in the eyes for a very long time.

"I was going to ask if you've ever been to one of these things before."

"I haven't." I look past her at the cheerleaders lining up, anxious for it to get started. "I'm excited. Do you always come?"

From meeting Oakleigh at That's Another Story, I never took her as the type of person to have much school spirit. She's not a sullen young woman, but she's very quiet and timid. The stands are bustling with activity and eagerness. I wouldn't have pictured her in the middle of it.

"I—umm."

I grin, knowing she's going to admit to having a crush on one of the athletes.

"I'm here to watch Lenny."

"Lenny?"

"The mascot," Kalen fills in when Oakleigh's cheeks flare red. "He's amazing."

"He really is," Oakleigh agrees readily.

The lights lower, casting a warm purple glow over the basketball court, and the crowd settles.

"Is Collins an athlete here?"

"Of sorts," he says, his eye mischievous, but he doesn't explain further.

"Is he around here?"

"Somewhere."

How weird is it that he doesn't point his cousin out? Maybe Collins is a walk-on athlete and not very good at whatever sport he plays.

I open my mouth to ask, but a loud boom draws my attention back to the pep rally.

The character, I can only assume is Lenny, powers through a wall of paper that's painted to look like bricks, and the crowd goes wild. Even Oakleigh claps her hands, cheering wildly. The lemur runs from one end of the gym to the other before doing back flips with twists and turns the entire length of the floor. By the time he makes it over to the cheerleaders and the gym is filled with a popular hip-hop song, everyone in the stands is on their feet, hollering how he's the best.

Lenny keeps perfect time with the cheerleaders as they dance to the song, and when they're done, I'm completely out of breath. A man with a gun couldn't pull the smile from my face at this point.

"This is amazing!" I yell loud enough for Kalen to hear me.

I take a moment to look around the arena, seeing everyone with smiles on their faces. Students and town residents from all walks of life are enthralled by the costumed lemur, and even in high school I never felt school spirit like this.

The dancing and gymnastics continue for several songs, and I realize quickly just how athletic everyone is. The cheerleaders pump everyone up, never getting red in the face or breathless. Lenny steals the show no matter what is going on around him, but then the music fades away. The crowd continues to cheer until a man walks out with a microphone urging Lenny away.

"Go on," the man says. "They won't listen to me so long as you're out here."

Lenny extravagantly bows at the waist for the audience before running back down to the end of the room.

"Lenny the Lemur, everyone!"

The crowd roars again as the man stands in the middle of the floor waiting for them to quiet down.

The man introduces himself as the dean of the athletic department, beginning his speech with thanking everyone for coming out and supporting the school, but I get lost watching Lenny sign autographs like a rock star for a gaggle of kids.

I can see why even a quiet girl like Oakleigh gets to her feet and cheers when he's around. I don't even know who's behind the mask and I want to fangirl a little and get him to sign something for me.

Chapter 24
Kalen

As always, Collins nailed his performance. He always does, but I know he gets nervous. All it would take is one wrong landing, a simple twist of his ankle and the entire jig would be up.

McKenna was just as entertained as everyone else in the stands. I told my cousin that Oakleigh had a Lenny sticker on her binder because every student does, but after watching her while she watched him, I know it's much more than that. I don't know if the girl has a furry fetish or what, but she's completely enraptured by Collins—er Lenny.

I smile at McKenna when she claps as Dean Rifkin introduces the football coach, but most of my attention is on Oakleigh. She's turned anxious since Lenny left the gym floor, and I know it's because the action she came for is over and she wants to leave. But she's the type of girl that would never insult someone by standing up and walking out of here before the entire thing is over. Her manners won't allow it.

During a break between speakers, Collins shows up in the stands his eyes wide and eager as he sees me. He's sweaty, his hair still wet near his temples. It's hot as blazes in that costume, but the smile on his face says he doesn't mind a bit. I nod, letting him know that he did an amazing job, something I can praise him for better at a different time when there aren't prying ears around. I know I'm going to tell McKenna the first chance I get because I know she won't tell anyone, but I don't want anyone else to figure it out.

Before Collins can make it to me fully, he spots Oakleigh, and like a dog smelling bacon, he diverts right to her.

"Hey, Oakleigh. Enjoying the pep rally?"

Oakleigh smiles before she realizes it's Collins, and I don't miss the way her eyes rake down the front of his sweaty shirt, pausing briefly on his biceps before her face turns into a frown.

I recognize the look. Not because Oakleigh ever looked at me that way, but because that look is the same one McKenna gave me before I finally won her over when she thought I—shudder—was dating or had dated Kristina and fathered Justin.

He may not see it, but Oakleigh is definitely interested in what she sees. I can only pray he doesn't mess it up completely before he can win her over. Knowing my cousin, there's going to be a lot of groveling in his future.

"That Lenny, huh? Amazing, right?"

Oakleigh shushes him as another coach takes the microphone to rave about his players. Collins, being smarter than I give him credit for, snaps his mouth closed as he takes a seat near Oakleigh but without touching her. He's using her inability to get up and walk out against her, and it should be sad, but I did it outside of the school at car pickup with McKenna.

The pep rally continues, each coach coming forward and praising their team. We've had an incredible year, but we always do. I hate that Collins only has one more year to be Lenny. He loves it, but there isn't a very big calling for mascots in the workforce. He wasn't very appreciative when I suggested Chuck E. Cheese.

I grimace thinking about that oversized rat. It's the thing of nightmares.

He keeps his head low, speaking during intermissions all the while Oakleigh stares straight ahead and ignores him. I'd give him an A plus for his determination, but eventually she's going to get tired of him. He needs to learn when to walk away and regroup.

"What?" Oakleigh hisses suddenly, standing to her full height to glare at him.

In the span of a blink, she grabs a soda from the girl in front of her and pours it over Collins' head before storming away.

The immediate area erupts in laughter, and I'm so stunned I can't even be bothered to look down at my shoes and the cold liquid soaking through to my socks.

When the laughter dies down, several girls offer him team towels—the ones they were using during the musical performance to wave in the air. Begrudgingly, he takes several, using them to wipe sticky soda from his hair.

I clap him on the shoulder when the entire thing is over, waiting right along with him while the stands begin to empty. I'd rather sit here and wait than join the crush of people trying to get to their cars.

"Tough luck, man."

"Whatever," he mutters.

"What did you say to her?"

"Hot teacher!" Collins says with a smile on his face that doesn't reach his eyes.

"Oh no," I hiss, standing to get between him and my girl. "Don't be a jerk because you messed up. What did you say to her anyway?"

"Nothing," he mutters as he looks around me toward McKenna.

We haven't spent much time in public because what we like to do most of these days are illegal outside of her house. Since neither one of us have any desire to get arrested for indecency, it means she hasn't met my cousin yet.

"I'm Collins Alexander. The better looking cousin." The dummy winks as he holds his hand out.

McKenna offers her hand to him, and I karate chop him at the wrist when he tries to lift it to his mouth.

"Fat chance, Romeo."

McKenna chuckles, and it brings a genuine smile to Collins' face.

"Better luck with the girl next time," McKenna says. "You should go to That's Another Story. She works there."

I wrap my arm around her, lucky that I get to walk out of here with this amazing woman.

"Or find another girl to hit on. That one can't stand you."

"Don't listen to him. She's interested. Just maybe don't push so hard. You want to get the girl not a restraining order."

Collins says his goodbyes as I turn McKenna in my arms.

"I'm starving," she whispers as I lower my mouth to hers.

"Feeling like some eggplant? All you can eat." I shift my hips against her, and she pays me back by twisting my nipple until I yelp.

"If you're talking about Ruth's down at the Brew and Chew, I'd say yes, but I don't think she was joking when she told us never to come back."

"Ruth loves me." I spin her around and escort her out of the stands. "Besides, Mom made eggplant parmesan."

"I've been dreaming about taking advantage of you in your childhood bedroom."

I hold her closer. "You know the rules. No ring no—"

She shuts me up with a kiss, whispering, "Then what are you waiting for?"

THE END

I hope you're as excited as I am about the stories to come in the Lindell world.

This small town is full of quirky folks just waiting for their stories to be told.

Although there was a lot of focus on Collins and Oakleigh, the Lindell Universe will launch with novels that take place in town and not at the University.

I figure the ones that have been waiting for true love the longest need their happily ever afters first!

I hope you tag along with me through the laughs (and sometimes tears) as these people navigate waters they've never pictured themselves swimming in.

Lindell debuts with <u>Back Against the Wall!</u>

Check out the synopsis!

A small town, single dad, enemies to lovers romance.

Crawling back to this small town was never in hockey star Chase Woodson's plans.

From hitting hockey pucks in front of thousands to selling urinal pucks at his father's hardware store, coming back home is his worst nightmare.

But being a (newly) single dad of twin boys means making sacrifices.

His boys need stability and his dad needs his help in the store.

Now he needs *her*.

Except, Chase has been the bane of Madison Kelly's existence since high school.

She just so happens to be the only available nanny in town.

Besides, high school was ten years ago.

People don't hold grudges that long, right?

OTHER BOOKS FROM MARIE JAMES

Blackbridge Security

Hostile Territory
Shot in the Dark
Contingency Plan
Truth Be Told
Calculated Risk
Heroic Measures
Sleight of Hand
Controlled Burn
Cease Fire
Crossing Borders

Blackbridge Security Box Set 1
Blackbridge Security Box Set 2
Blackbridge Security Box Set 3

Standalones

Crowd Pleaser
Macon
We Said Forever
More Than a Memory

Mission Mercenaries Series
Lessons Learned
Mistakes Made
Bridges Burned
Depravity Delivered
Redemption Refused

Cole Brothers Series
Love Me Like That
Teach Me Like That

Cerberus MC

Kincaid: Cerberus MC Book 1
Kid: Cerberus MC Book 2
Shadow: Cerberus MC Book 3
Dominic: Cerberus MC Book 4
Snatch: Cerberus MC Book 5
Lawson: Cerberus MC Book 6
Hound: Cerberus MC Book 7
Griffin: Cerberus MC Book 8
Samson: Cerberus MC Book 9
Tug: Cerberus MC Book 10
Scooter: Cerberus MC Book 11
Cannon: Cerberus MC Book 12
Rocker: Cerberus MC Book 13
Colton: Cerberus MC Book 14
Drew: Cerberus MC Book 15
Jinx: Cerberus MC Book 16
Thumper: Cerberus MC Book 17
Apollo: Cerberus MC Book 18
Legend: Cerberus MC Book 19
Grinch: Cerberus MC Book 20
Harley: Cerberus MC Book 21
A Very Cerberus Christmas
Landon: Cerberus MC Book 22
Spade: Cerberus MC Book 23
Aro: Cerberus MC Book 24
Boomer: Cerberus MC Book 25
Ugly: Cerberus MC Book 26
Bishop: Cerberus MC Book 27

Legacy: Cerberus MC Book 28
Stormy: Cerberus MC Book 29
Oracle: Cerberus MC Book 30
Newton: Cerberus MC Book 31

Cerberus MC Box Set 1
Cerberus MC Box Set 2
Cerberus MC Box Set 3
Cerberus MC Box Set 4
Cerberus MC Box Set 5
Cerberus MC Box Set 6
Cerberus MC Box Set 7
Cerberus MC Box Set 8

Ravens Ruin MC
Desperate Beginnings: Prequel
Grab it for free HERE!

Book 1: Sins of the Father
Book 2: Luck of the Devil
Book 3: Dancing with the Devil

MM Romance
Grinder
Taunting Tony

Westover Prep Series
(bully/enemies to lovers romance)
One-Eighty
Catch Twenty-Two

Hale Series
Coming to Hale
Begging for Hale
Hot as Hale
To Hale and Back

Lindell
Back Against the Wall
Easier Said than Done

Made in the USA
Columbia, SC
29 November 2023

26797902R00089